"NUMBER NINETY"

"Number Ninety"

& Other Ghost Stories

by

B. M. Croker

Swan River Press
Dublin, Ireland
MMXIX

"Number Ninety"
by B. M. Croker

Published by
Swan River Press
Dublin, Ireland
in October MMXXI

www.swanriverpress.ie
brian@swanriverpress.ie

Cover design by Meggan Kehrli
from cover artwork by Alan Corbett

Set in Garamond by Ken Mackenzie

Published with assistance from Dublin UNESCO
City of Literature and Dublin City Libraries

ISBN 978-1-78380-753-6

Swan River Press published
a limited hardback edition of
"Number Ninety" in August 2019.

Contents

❀

Introduction

Many years ago, while collecting the first editions of Bram Stoker, my heart would often leap when apparently spotting his rarely encountered name in dimly lit alcoves of second-hand bookshops, only to find that I had actually misread the similar gilt lettering of "B. M. Croker". Having no special taste for this other writer's Indian or Irish romances, I usually disregarded them.

At that time B. M. Croker was only remembered (by a shrinking number of admirers) as a once-popular bestselling novelist. Her supernatural tales had sunk into total neglect, and none had ever been revived in anthologies (not even by Hugh Lamb or Peter Haining).

I first became aware of her ghost stories after buying the first two volumes of *Chapman's Magazine of Fiction* (May to December 1895) in the original cloth richly decorated by Walter Crane. The Christmas Number contained a fine array of weird tales including "The Story of a Ghost" by Violet Hunt, "The Red Hand" by Arthur Machen, "The Case of Euphemia Raphash" by M. P. Shiel, and "Number Ninety" by Mrs. B. M. Croker.

I eventually reprinted this latter tale (Croker's debut in any genre anthology) in the first of my six Christmas anthologies, *Ghosts for Christmas* (Michael O'Mara, 1988).

I then researched her bibliography which amounted to 49 titles (42 novels and 7 short story collections), of which only a small fraction were listed in her *Who's Who* entry, and gradually unearthed all the very scarce collections which had remained out-of-print for nearly seventy years and contained a surprisingly good variety of ghost stories.

Like "Number Ninety", several of the other tales were set specifically in the Christmas period—obviously designed for late Victorian and Edwardian Christmas Numbers—and most had a higher "macabre" and grisly content than was usual at that time in seasonal weird tales, especially when compared to Mrs. Oliphant, Mrs. Molesworth, and Mrs. Henry Wood.

Apart from "Number Ninety", the only other Croker ghost story to reach a wide audience in the past decade has been "To Let", reprinted in both the Oxford Anthology *Victorian Ghost Stories* (1991) and Reader's Digest's *Great Ghost Stories* (1997) which stated that "her novels have not stood the test of time, but her shorter fiction is as enjoyable today as when it was first written, providing a vivid insight into the day-to-day lives of the British in India."

B. M. Croker was one of the most popular and best-known novelists in the English-speaking world over a forty-year period, and is very well documented. Like several of her equally busy contemporaries, notably L. T. Meade, Rosa Mulholland, and Mrs. J. H. Riddell, she came from an old-established Irish family.

Bithia Mary Sheppard was born circa 1849, the only daughter of Rev. William Sheppard, Rector of Kilgefin, Co. Roscommon, who died suddenly seven years later. (The old family home at Ballanagare still survives today, though roofless.) She was educated at Rockferry, Cheshire, and at Tours in France. Her favourite recreations were riding and reading.

In 1871 she married John Stokes Croker, an officer in the 21st Royal Scots and Munster Fusiliers. His family, the Crokers of Bally Maguarde, Co. Limerick, claimed direct descent from Sir John Croker, standard bearer to King Edward IV.

Following common tradition as a Victorian soldier's wife, Bithia accompanied her husband to India, where he served for several years in Madras and Burma. They had one child, Gertrude Eileen (always called "Eileen"). They later lived in Bengal, and at a hill-station in Wellington (where many of her early stories were written), very similar to the one described in "To Let".

After the first ten years of marriage and motherhood, she began writing novels and short stories (like "The Ghost in the Dâk Bungalow" for *London Society* in 1882) to occupy the long hot days while her husband was away. Always a keen sportsman, he enjoyed a great deal of big game shooting.

Both the writing and eventual publication of her first two novels, *Proper Pride* and *Pretty Miss Neville*, with her young daughter Eileen's providential rescue of the manuscript from the flames, were humorously described by Mrs. Croker in her interview with Helen Black, which is reproduced in the appendix to the present volume.

Proper Pride (Ward & Downey, 1882), the first of her long series of Anglo-Indian romances to be published, was also her only novel to appear anonymously. The story has some lively military chapters set in Afghanistan, based directly on her husband's exploits.

Pretty Miss Neville, published in three volumes by Tinsley in 1883, was the first of her novels—directly credited to "B. M. Croker"—to attract widespread attention; and among its most distinguished admirers was Prime Minister W. E. Gladstone, who was seen to be absorbed in its pages while seated on the front bench in the House of Commons! This compulsive tale is narrated by the title-character, a faithless coquette in the Indian station of Mukkapore.

All her eleven lengthy novels from *Pretty Miss Neville* up to *A Third Person* and *Married or Single?* (both 1895) were published in the traditional "three-decker" format (@ 31/6), before passing quickly into a series of one-volume reprints priced @ 6/-, 5/-, 2/6, 2/-, 1/-and 6d. *Proper Pride* and *Pretty Miss Neville* reached their 6th and 5th editions respectively by 1887, a sure sign of their great popularity.

Colonel Croker was on half-pay in the mid-80s, so the money his wife received from London publishers was undoubtedly welcome to ensure a comfortable existence in the confined circles of upper-class colonial life so accurately described in her stories.

After two novels for Sampson Low—*Some One Else* (1885) and *A Bird of Passage* (1886), the latter set in the Andaman Islands, where the Crokers lived for several months—she achieved her greatest success to date with *Diana Barrington: A Romance of Central India* (Ward & Downey, 1888), another rousing story of Anglo-Indian life in a military station, which drew on the author's close intimacy with Irish character as well as her sympathetic knowledge of the Indian native.

For her time, Mrs. Croker was always unusually sympathetic to the India native population, as one reviewer of *Diana Barrington* observed: "She does not regard the natives as 'niggers' but bears eloquent testimony to their courtesy, chivalry and charity."

Any Englishman in a Croker tale who displayed antipathy or insulting behaviour towards a native Indian was sure to be a villain, and (especially in her ghost stories) eventually met their macabre just deserts.

Many of her novels contrived to have a strong Irish (rather than Anglo)-Indian connection, as in three sagas for F. V. White: *Two Masters* (1890), *Interference* (1891), and *A Third*

Person (1895). *Interference*, which was serialised in *Belgravia* magazine throughout 1891, begins with fox-hunting in Ireland and ends with husband-hunting at an Indian hill-station, with many calamities and misunderstandings in between.

As virtually every family in late-Victorian Britain had at least one member serving in either Ireland or India, the great majority of readers could enjoy and identify with Mrs. Croker's highly entertaining and fast-moving blockbusters.

On her husband's retirement in 1892 (at the age of 47), the Crokers went to live at Lordello in Co. Wicklow (south of Dublin), a picturesque setting well described by Helen C. Black in her interview published four years later in *Pen, Pencil, Baton and Mask* (Spottiswoode, 1896).

Having worked haphazardly with a literary agent and four different publishers at long-distance from India, Mrs. Croker was now able to settle more securely with two regular publishers, the old-established fiction factory Chatto & Windus, and the much newer firm of Methuen.

With Chatto & Windus she published *A Family Likeness: A Sketch in the Himalayas* (1892), *Mr. Jervis: A Romance of the Indian Hills* (1894), *The Real Lady Hilda* (1896), *Beyond the Pale* (1897), *Miss Balmain's Past* (1898), *Infatuation* (1899), *Terence* (1899; with six plates by Sidney Paget), *The Cat's-Paw* (1902; with twelve plates by Fred Pegram), and *The Spanish Necklace* (1907; with eight plates by Fred Pegram). These were all perennial bestsellers, and had renewed life for another twenty or thirty years as large mass-market paperbacks. Their wonderfully evocative and colourful pictorial covers can be seen prominently displayed in *Sixpenny Wonderfuls* (Chatto & Windus/Hogarth Press, 1985), a survey of Chatto's "6d gems from the past" alongside Ouida, Walter Besant, Wilkie Collins, and other great names.

Besides reviving some of her earliest successes (*Proper Pride; Pretty Miss Neville, Diana Barrington*) as sixpenny paperbacks, Chatto & Windus also published four collections of short stories by B. M. Croker in quick succession: *"To Let"* (1893), *Village Tales and Jungle Tragedies* (1895; later reprinted as *Jungle Tales*), *In the Kingdom of Kerry* (1896), and *Jason* (1899), all issued in both 3/6 cloth and 2/- yellowback (pictorial boards) editions.

"To Let" is by far the strongest of these collections in supernatural and ghostly content. The title-story originally appeared in the 1890 Christmas Number of *London Society*. The dramatic picture on the yellowback cover shows the imminent murder of Gordon Forbes by two natives, as witnessed by Julia and Nellie in the ghostly vision in "The Dâk Bungalow at Dakor".

The stories in *"To Let"* were set mainly in India, or the surrounding ocean (like "The Former Passengers"), whereas *In the Kingdom of Kerry* concentrates much more on Ireland (as indicated by the title) with only an occasional foray to India ("Her Last Wishes").

During her years in Co. Wicklow, Mrs. Croker naturally specialised much more on novels set in her native Ireland, notably *Beyond the Pale* (1897, first serialised in *The Times*) which featured a horsey Irish heroine, "Galloping Jerry". This amusing narrative of country life in Munster, sketching the peasants and broken-down gentry without going very deeply into the Irish temperament or throwing much light on Irish troubles and politics, was very typical of her work at this period.

Terence (1899), a Kerry romance in which a rich Australian girl falls in love with the bankrupt heir of the once princely house of Desmond, was subsequently dramatised by the author herself with a fair measure of success. It ran for two years in America.

Methuen, her other regular publisher, brought out two further Croker collections of short stories, *A State Secret*

(1901) and *The Old Cantonment* (1905), and several novels:
Married or Single? (1895: her final three-decker), *Peggy of
the Bartons* (1898; an English country idyll which ran
into numerous editions), *Angel* (1901; an Anglo-Indian
romance), *Johanna* (1903), *The Happy Valley* (1904), *A Nine
Days' Wonder* (1905), *Katherine the Arrogant* (1909), and
Babes in the Wood (1910). Several of these, like *Johanna* and
A Nine Days' Wonder, were Irish stories.

Following the example of Chatto & Windus, Mrs.
Croker's novels for Methuen, alongside those of S. Bar-
ing-Gould, Marie Corelli, Robert Hichens, et al., were
(according to Maureen Duffy in her centenary history of
Methuen, *A Thousand Capricious Chances*) "often appearing
simultaneously at six shillings, two shillings and sixpence,
one shilling, sevenpence, and in the monthly sixpenny
Novelist. There was still at this period no real rival to the
novel for leisure pastime, and women in particular, who
were much more restricted in their activities than men,
read avidly. The only true alternatives to fiction were the
theatre and the music hall".

With huge sales and continuing royalties, it was not unusual for Mrs. Croker to earn as much as £2,000 for a single
novel at the turn of the century. Robert Lee Wolff unearthed
the author's extant correspondence with her literary agent,
Morris Colles, which shows that she received £1,650 for
The Spanish Necklace (1907), running to 100,000 words.

In 1897 the Crokers moved from Ireland to their final
home at 5 Radnor Cliff, Sandgate, near Folkestone in Kent.
While his wife continued her prolific literary career, Colonel
Croker enjoyed local club life and various sports. Always
an enthusiastic fisherman, he visited Norway annually on
angling expeditions. He died at home on 27 June 1911.

Now in her sixties, B. M. Croker carried on writing
at least one novel each year without a break. She took an

active role in the Radnor Club and various literary societies, and was a regular hostess to visiting writers. Ghost-hunter Elliott O'Donnell stayed with her in Sandgate when he proposed "that psychic phenomena or ghosts prove that there is an after-life for animals as well as for man", in a debate for the Folkestone, Dover & District Debating Society on 26 January 1914.

She gradually shifted away from Methuen and Chatto to Hurst & Blackett (*The Youngest Miss Mowbray*, 1906; *The Company's Servant*, 1907), Mills & Boon (*Fame,* 1910), F. V. White (*A Rolling Stone*, 1911), Cassell (*Quicksands*, 1915; *The Road to Mandalay*, 1917); and during her last decade—seven more novels were published by Hutchinson: *The Serpent's Tooth* (1912), *In Old Madras* (1913), *Lismoyle: An Example in Ireland* (1914), *Given in Marriage* (1916), *A Rash Experiment* (1917), *Bridget* (1918) and *Blue China* (1919), plus one final collection with two horrific ghost stories: *Odds and Ends* (1919).

In that same year (1919), at the age of seventy, Mrs. Croker was contracted by Cassell for another three novels—*The Pagoda Tree* (1919), *The Chaperon* (1920), and *The House of Rest* (1921) and in the late summer of 1920, she signed another contract with Hutchinson for her next three books, which were never written.

After a short period of illness (probably related to the influenza epidemic), she was taken to a nursing home at 30 Dorset Square in London where she died suddenly on 20 October 1920.

The perceptive *Times* obituary writer commented (22 October) on B. M. Croker's amazingly productive career: "Much of her success was due to her sympathy with youth, her quick sense of humour untainted by vulgarity, and the skill with which she contrived to hold her public's interest in her stories. Perhaps, also, a part of the secret of her popularity was the frank enjoyment she derived from her work and her genuine interest in her own creations—the surest medium, in clever, honest hands, of capturing the interest of readers. While never malicious, she made full use of her knowledge of human nature, which, added to unusual powers of observation, a retentive memory, and a ready vocabulary, formed a valuable equipment for one of her profession. One of the outstanding features of her work was that, though her methods retained the flavour of the old 'three-decker' type of romance, her novels were always up to date, missing nothing of social changes and progress. Many successful writers of yesterday and today owe thanks to her for her kindly advice, encouragement, and help during their early struggles; jealousy was not in her nature, and her generous admiration for all of the best in other people's efforts was one of her many fine characteristics. In her youth she was a good rider, and in her old age she remained a true sportswoman in every sense of the term. Her daughter, Mrs. Albert Whitaker, is said to have been the model from which she drew the portraits of some of her beautiful heroines."

In her will she left effects of £8421.10s.9d. to her daughter Mrs. Gertrude Eileen Whitaker and grandson Captain John Albert Charles Whitaker.

Eileen had married (in 1896) businessman Albert Edward Whitaker, who was knighted in 1926 and created a baronet in 1936. The family estate is at Babworth Hall, Retford, Nottinghamshire. Captain (later Major-General) John Whitaker (1897-1957) succeeded his father to the baronetcy in 1945. His three sons are Sir James Whitaker, 3rd Bt., Rev. David Whitaker, and Ben Whitaker, Labour MP for Hampstead 1966-70 and the writer of over a dozen books including *The Police* and *Parks for People*.

Coming full circle, David Whitaker has followed his great-grandmother's example by writing several ghost stories, published as *In Face of Fear* (Avon Books, 1998). The present collection begins with the London setting of "Number Ninety", preserving the original text from *Chapman's Magazine of Fiction* (Christmas 1895), rather than the modified version retitled "An Unexpected Invitation" in *A State Secret* (1901) which deleted all references to "Ninety". This may have been enforced by infuriated Londoners who happened to reside in very similar houses with the same number!

We then move to an equally weird location off southeast Asia on a very spooky sea voyage, en route for India with a further six macabre and touching ghost stories set in the familiar surroundings of Croker's Indian hinterland with its remote dâk bungalows and hill-stations. The next four tales are situated further afield in Scotland, Australia, and America.

After these twelve ghost stories, we move finally to France with two supernatural yarns dealing with reincarnation, possession and the transmigration of souls, and to Ireland with the uncanny precognition of "Mrs. Ponsonby's Dream". (The same theme and Irish location was also used by Mrs. Croker in "The Red Woollen Necktie", which I revived in *Enigmatic Tales*, No. 3, December 1998.)

Several more macabre though non-supernatural tales can be found in B. M. Croker's collections, ranging from the superstition of "Thirteen" and "The Little Brass God" to the murder by decapitation in "Jack Straw's Castle".

While the name of this greatly talented writer has been unjustly neglected for too long, another character of the same nomenclature came briefly into prominence earlier this year in the BBC TV serial *The Ghost Hunter,* starring a wonderfully manic Jean Marsh in the title-role—as "Mrs. Croker"!

Richard Dalby
Scarborough
January 2000

"Number Ninety"

"Number Ninety"

"To let furnished, for a term of years, at a very low rental, a large old-fashioned family residence, comprising eleven bed-rooms, four reception-rooms, dressing-rooms, two staircases, complete servants' offices, ample accommodation for a gentleman's establishment, including six-stall stable, coach-house, etc."

The above advertisement referred to Number Ninety. For a period extending over some years this notice appeared spasmodically in the various daily papers. Occasionally you saw it running for a week or a fortnight at a stretch, as if it were resolved to force itself into consideration by sheer persistency. Sometimes for months I looked for it in vain. Other ignorant folk might possibly fancy that the efforts of the house-agent had been at last crowned with success—that it was let, and no longer in the market.

I knew better. I knew that it would never, never find a tenant as long as oak and ash endured. I knew that it was passed on as a hopeless case, from house-agent to house-agent. I knew that it would never be occupied, save by rats—and, more than this, I knew the reason why!

I will not say in what square, street, or road Number Ninety may be found, nor will I divulge to human being its precise and exact locality, but this I'm prepared to state, that it is positively in existence, is in London, and is still empty.

3

❊

Twenty years ago, this very Christmas, my friend John Hollyoak (civil engineer) and I were guests at a bachelor's party; partaking, in company with eight other celibates, of a very *recherché* little dinner, in the neighbourhood of Piccadilly. Conversation became very brisk as the champagne circulated, and many topics were started, discussed, and dismissed.

They (I say *they* advisedly, as I myself am a man of few words) talked on an extraordinary variety of subjects.

I distinctly recollect a long argument on mushrooms—mushrooms, murders, racing, cholera; from cholera we came to sudden death, from sudden death to churchyards and from churchyards, it was naturally but a step to ghosts.

On this last topic the arguments became fast and furious, for the company was divided into two camps. The larger, "the opposition", who scoffed, sneered, and snapped their fingers, and laughed with irritating contempt at the very name of ghosts, was headed by John Hollyoak; the smaller party, who were dogged, angry, and prepared to back their opinions to any extent, had for their leader our host, a bald-headed man of business, whom I certainly would have credited (as I mentally remarked) with more sense.

The believers in the supernatural obtained a hearing, so far as to relate one or two blood-curdling, first or second-hand experiences, which, when concluded, instead of being received with an awe-struck and respectful silence, were pooh-poohed, with shouts of laughter, and taunting suggestions that were by no means complimentary to the intelligence, or sobriety, of the victims of superstition. Argument and counter-argument, waxed louder and hotter, and there was every prospect of a very stormy conclusion to the evening's entertainment.

John Hollyoak, who was the most vehement, most incredulous, the most jocular, and most derisive of the anti-ghost faction, brought matters to a climax by declaring that nothing would give him greater satisfaction than to pass a night in a haunted house—and the worse its character, the better he would be pleased!

His challenge was instantly taken up by our somewhat ruffled host, who warmly assured him that his wishes could be easily satisfied, and that he would be accommodated with a night's lodging in a haunted house within twenty-four hours—in fact, in a house of such a desperate reputation, that even the adjoining mansions stood vacant.

He then proceeded to give a brief outline of the history of Number Ninety. It had once been the residence of a well-known county family, but what evil events had happened therein tradition did not relate.

On the death of the last owner—a diabolical-looking aged person, much resembling the typical wizard—it had passed into the hands of a kinsman, resident abroad, who had no wish to return to England, and who desired his agents to let it, if they could—a most significant proviso!

Year by year went by, and still this "Highly desirable family mansion" could find no tenant, although the rent was reduced, and reduced, and again reduced, to almost zero!

The most ghastly whispers were afloat—the most terrible experiences were actually proclaimed on the housetops!

No tenant would remain, even *gratis*; and for the last ten years, this "handsome, desirable town family residence" had been the abode of rats by day, and something else by night—so said the neighbours.

Of course it offered the very thing for John, and he snatched up the gauntlet on the spot. He scoffed at its evil repute, and solemnly promised to rehabilitate its character within a week.

It was in vain that he was solemnly warned—that one of his fellow guests gravely assured him "that he would not pass a night in Number Ninety for ninety thousand pounds—it would be the price of his reason."

"You value your reason at a very high figure," replied John, with an indulgent smile. "I will venture mine for nothing."

"Those laugh who win," put in our host sharply. "You have not been through the wood yet, though your name is Hollyoak! I invite all present to dine with me in three days from this; and then, if our friend here has proved that he has got the better of the spirits, we will all laugh together. Is that a bargain?"

This invitation was promptly accepted by the whole company; and then they fell to making practical arrangements for John's lodging for the next night.

I had no actual hand—or, more properly speaking, tongue—in this discussion, which carried us on till a late hour; but nevertheless, the next night at ten o'clock—for no ghost with any self-respect would think of appearing before that time—I found myself standing, as John's second, on the steps of the notorious abode; but I was not going to remain; the hansom that brought us was to take me back to my own respectable chambers.

The ill-fated house was large, solemn-looking, and gloomy. A heavy portico frowned down on neighbouring bare-faced hall-doors. The caretaker (an army pensioner, bravest of the brave in daylight) was prudently awaiting us outside with a key, which said key he turned in the lock, and admitted us into a great echoing hall, black as Erebus, saying as he did so: "My missus has haired the bed, and made up a good fire in the first front, sir. Your things is all laid hout, and" (dubiously to John) "I hope you'll have a comfortable night, sir. No, sir! Thank you, sir! Excuse me, I'll not come in! Good-night!" and with the words still on his lips, he clattered down the steps with most indecent haste, and—vanished.

"And of course you will not come in either," said John. "It is not in the bond, and I prefer to face them alone!" and he laughed contemptuously, a laugh that had a curious echo, it struck me at the time. A laugh strangely repeated, with an unpleasant mocking emphasis.

"Call for me, alive or dead, at eight o'clock tomorrow morning!" he added, pushing me forcibly out into the porch, and closing the door with a heavy, reverberating clang, that sounded half-way down the street.

I did call for him the next morning as desired, with the army pensioner, who stared as his commonplace, self-possessed appearance, with an expression of respectful astonishment.

"So it was all humbug, of course," I said, as he took my arm, and we set off for our club.

"You shall have the whole story whenever we have had something to eat," he replied somewhat impatiently. "It will keep till after breakfast—I'm famishing!"

I remarked that he looked unusually grave as we chatted over our broiled fish and omelette, and that occasionally his attention seemed wandering, to say the least of it. The moment he had brought out his cigar-case and lit up he turned to me and said:

"I see you are just quivering to know my experience, and I won't keep you on tenter-hooks any longer. In four words—I have seen them!"

I am (as before hinted) a silent man. I merely looked at him with widely-parted mouth and staring interrogative eyes.

I believe I had best endeavour to give the narrative without comment, and in John Hollyoak's own way. This is, as well as I can recollect, his experience word for word:—

"I proceeded upstairs, after I had shut you out, lighting my way by a match, and found the front room easily,

7

as the door was ajar, and it was lit up by a roaring and most cheerful-looking fire, and two wax candles. It was a comfortable apartment, furnished with old-fashioned chairs and tables, and the traditional four-poster. There were numerous doors, which proved to be cupboards; and when I had executed a rigorous search in each of these closets and locked them, and investigated the bed above and beneath, sounded the walls, and bolted the door, I sat down before the fire, lit a cigar, opened a book, and felt that I was going to be master of the situation, and most thoroughly and comfortably 'at home'. My novel proved absorbing. I read on greedily, chapter after chapter, and so interested was I, and amused—for it was a lively book—that I positively lost sight of my whereabouts, and fancied myself reading in my own chamber! There was not a sound—not even a mouse in the wainscot. The coals dropping from the grate occasionally broke the silence, till a neighbouring church-clock slowly boomed twelve! '*The hour!*' I said to myself, with a laugh, as I gave the fire a rousing poke, and commenced a fresh chapter; but ere I had read three pages, I had occasion to pause and listen. What was that distinct sound now coming nearer and nearer? 'Rats, of course,' said Common-sense—'it was just the house for vermin.' Then a longish silence. Again a stir, sounds approaching, as if apparently caused by many feet passing down the corridor—high-heeled shoes, the sweeping swish of silken trains! Of course it was all imagination, I assured myself—or rats! Rats were capable of making such improbable noises!

"Then another silence. No sound but cinders and the ticking of my watch, which I had laid upon the table.

"I resumed my book, rather ashamed, and a little in-dignant with myself for having neglected it, and calmly dismissed my late interruption as 'rats—nothing but rats'.

"I had been reading and smoking for some time in a placid and highly incredulous frame of mind, when I was somewhat rudely startled by a loud single-knock at my room door. I took no notice of it, but merely laid down my novel and sat tight. Another knock more imperious this time. After a moment's mental deliberation I arose, armed myself with the poker, prepared to brain any number of rats, and threw the door open with a violent swing that strained its very hinges, and beheld, to my amazement, a tall powdered footman in a laced scarlet livery, who, making a formal inclination of his head, astonished me still further by saying:

" 'Dinner is ready!'

" 'I'm not coming!' I replied, without a moment's hesitation, and thereupon I slammed the door in his face, locked it, and resumed my seat, also my book; but reading was a farce; my ears were aching for the next sound.

"It came soon—rapid steps running up the stairs, and again a single knock. I went over to the door, and once more discovered the tall footman, who repeated, with a studied courtesy:

" 'Dinner is ready, and the company are waiting.'

" 'I told you I was not coming. Be off, and be hanged to you!' I cried again, shutting the door violently.

"This time I did not make even a pretence at reading, I merely sat and waited for the next move.

"I had not long to sit. In ten minutes I heard a third loud summons. I rose, went to the door, and tore it open. There, as I expected, was the servant again, with his parrot speech:

" 'Dinner is ready, the company are waiting, and the master says you must come!'

" 'All right, then, I'll come,' I replied, wearied by reason of his importunity, and feeling suddenly fired with a desire to see the end of the adventure.

"He accordingly led the way downstairs, and I followed him, noting as I went the gilt buttons on his coat, and his splendidly turned calves, also that the hall and passages were now brilliantly illuminated, and that several liveried servants were passing to and fro, and that from—presumably—the dining-room, there issued a buzz of tongues, loud volleys of laughter, many hilarious voices, and a clatter of knives and forks. I was not left much time for speculation, as in another second I found myself inside the door, and my escort announced me in a stentorian voice as 'Mr. Hollyoak'.

"I could hardly credit my senses, as I looked round and saw about two dozen people, dressed in a fashion of the last century, seated at the table, which was loaded with gold and silver plate, and lighted by a blaze of wax candles in massive candelabra.

"A swarthy elderly gentleman, who presided at the head of the board, rose deliberately as I entered. He was dressed in a crimson coat, braided with silver. He wore a purple peruke, had the most piercing black eyes I ever encountered, made me the finest bow I ever received in all my life, and with a polite wave of a taper hand, indicated my seat—a vacant chair between two powdered and patched beauties, with overflowing white shoulders and necks sparkling with diamonds.

"At first I was fully convinced that the whole affair was a superbly-matured practical joke. Everything looked so real, so truly flesh and blood, so complete in every detail; but I gazed around in vain for one familiar face.

"I saw young, old, and elderly; handsome and the reverse. On all faces there was a similar expression—reckless, hardened defiance, and something else that made me shudder, but that I could not classify or define.

"Were they a secret community? Burglars or coiners? But no; in one rapid glance I noticed that they belonged exclusively to the upper stratum of society—bygone society.

The jabber of talking had momentarily ceased, and the host, imperiously hammering the table with a knife-handle, said in a singularly harsh grating voice:

" 'Ladies and gentlemen, permit me to give you a toast! "Our guest!" ' looking straight at me with his glittering coal-black eyes.

"Every glass was immediately raised. Twenty faces were turned towards mine, when, happily, a sudden impulse seized me. I sprang to my feet and said:

" 'Ladies and gentlemen, I beg to thank you for your kind hospitality, but before I accept it, allow me to say grace!'

"I did not wait for permission, but hurriedly repeated a Latin benediction. Ere the last syllable was uttered, in an instant there was a violent crash, an uproar, a sound of running, of screams, groans and curses, and then utter darkness.

"I found myself standing alone by the big mahogany table which I could just dimly discern with the aid of a street-lamp, that threw its meagre rays into the great empty dining-room from the other side of the area.

"I must confess that I felt my nerves a little shaken by this instantaneous change from light to darkness—from a crowd of gay and noisy companions, to utter solitude and silence. I stood for a moment trying to recover my mental balance. I rubbed my eyes hard to assure myself that I was wide awake, and then I placed this very cigar-case in the middle of the table, as a sign and token that I had been downstairs—which cigar-case I found exactly where I left it this morning—and then went and groped my way into the hall and regained my room.

"I met with no obstruction *en route*. I saw no one, but as I closed and double-locked my door I distinctly heard a low laugh outside the keyhole—a sort of suppressed, malicious titter, that made me furious.

11

"I opened the door at once. There was nothing to be seen. I waited and listened—dead silence. I then undressed and went to bed, resolved that a whole army of footmen would fail to allure me once more to that festive board. I was determined not to lose my night's rest—ghosts or no ghosts.

"Just as I was dozing off I remember hearing the neighbouring clock chime two. It was the last sound I was aware of; the house was now as silent as a vault. My fire burnt away cheerfully. I was no longer in the least degree inclined for reading, and I fell fast asleep and slept soundly till I heard the cabs and milk-carts beginning their morning career.

"I then rose, dressed at my leisure, and found you, my good, faithful friend, awaiting me, rather anxiously, on the hall-doorsteps.

"I have not done with that house yet. I'm determined to find out who these people are, and where they come from. I shall sleep there again tonight, and so shall 'Crib', my bulldog; and you will see that I shall have news for you tomorrow morning—if I am alive to tell the tale," he added with a laugh.

In vain I would have dissuaded him. I protested, argued, and implored. I declared that rashness was not courage; that he had seen enough; that I, who had seen nothing, and only listened to his experiences, was convinced that Number Ninety was a house to be avoided.

I might just as well have talked to my umbrella! So, once more, I reluctantly accompanied him to his previous night's lodging. Once more I saw him swallowed up inside the gloomy, forbidding-looking, re-echoing hall.

I then went home in an unusually anxious, semi-excited, nervous state of mind; and I, who generally outrival the Seven Sleepers, lay wide awake, tumbling and tossing hour after hour, a prey to the most foolish ideas—ideas I would have laughed to scorn in daylight.

More than once I was certain that I heard John Hollyoak distractedly calling me; and I sat up in bed and listened intently. Of course it was fancy, for the instant I did so, there was no sound.

At the first gleam of winter dawn, I rose, dressed, and swallowed a cup of good strong coffee to clear my brain from the misty notions it had harboured during the night. And then I invested myself in my warmest topcoat and comforter, and set off for Number Ninety. Early as it was— it was but half-past seven—I found the army pensioner was before me, pacing the pavement with a countenance that would have made a first-rate frontispiece for Burton's *Anatomy of Melancholy*—a countenance the reverse of cheerful!

I was not disposed to wait for eight o'clock. I was too uneasy, and too impatient for further particulars of the dinner-party. So I rang with all my might, and knocked with all my main.

No sound within—no answer! But John was always a heavy sleeper. I was resolved to arouse him all the same, and knocked and rang, and rang and knocked, incessantly for fully ten minutes.

I then stooped down and applied my eye to the keyhole; I looked steadily into the aperture, till I became accustomed to the darkness, and then it seemed to me that another eye—a very strange, fiery eye—was glaring into mine from the other side of the door!

I removed my eye and applied my mouth instead, and shouted with all the power of my lungs (I did not care a straw if passers-by took me for an escaped lunatic):

"John! John! Hollyoak!"

How his name echoed and re-echoed up through that great empty house! "He must hear *that*," I said to myself as I pressed my ear closely against the lock, and listened with throbbing suspense.

The echo of "Hollyoak" had hardly died away when I swear that I distinctly heard a low, sniggering, mocking laugh—*that* was my only answer—that; and a vast unresponsive silence.

I was now quite desperate. I shook the door frantically, with all my strength. I broke the bell; in short, my behaviour was such that it excited the curiosity of a policeman, who crossed the road to know "What was up?"

"I want to get in!" I panted, breathless with my exertions.

"You'd better stay where you are!" said Bobby; "the outside of this house is the best of it! There are terrible stories—"

"But there is a gentleman inside it!" I interrupted impatiently. "He slept there last night, and I can't wake him. He has the key!"

"Oh, you can't *wake* him!" returned the policeman gravely. "Then we must get a locksmith!"

But already the thoughtful pensioner had procured one; and already a considerable and curious crowd surrounded the steps.

After five minutes of (to me) maddening delay, the great heavy door was opened, and swung slowly back, and I instantly rushed in, followed less precipitately by the policeman and pensioner.

I had not far to seek John Hollyoak! He and his dog were lying at the foot of the stairs, both stone dead!

The Former Passengers

"Who is whispering and calling through the rain?
  Far above the tempest crashing,
  And the torrent's ceaseless dashing,
  I hear a weary calling, as of pain."

"If any one can help you, it will be Captain Blane." This sentence was uttered by a smart young clerk, in a shipping office in Rangoon, who, clothed in cool white drill, leant his elbows confidentially on the desk, and concluded his speech with a reassuring nod.

I was *en route* from Upper Burmah to Singapore, in order to attend my sister's wedding. Our flat river-boat was late, and when I presented myself at the booking-office of the P. and O., I found to my dismay that the steamer for the Straits had sailed at dawn, and that there would not be another for a week! I was therefore bound to miss the wedding, and waste my precious leave in Rangoon, thanks to the leisurely old tub that had dawdled down from Mandalay.

I turned my eyes expectantly on Captain Blane, a short-necked, weather-beaten sailor, in a blue serge coat with gilt buttons, and a peaked cap. He surveyed me steadily, with a pair of small keen eyes, and evidently did not receive the suggestion with enthusiasm.

"We don't carry passengers," he announced in a gruff voice. "My ship is only a cargo-boat, a tramp; and we have no accommodation whatsoever."

"No accommodation!" echoed the clerk, incredulously. "Oh, I say, come!"

"Why, you know very well that all the cabins are chock-full of cargo; and we have never carried a passenger since I took command."

"If there was any hole or corner where you could stow me, I don't mind how I rough it," I urged; "and I'll pay full first-class fare."

"Oh, there's lots of holes and corners," admitted the captain. "And you'd just get the ship's rations, same as the officers and myself; no soups and entrées—plain roast and boiled."

"I'm not particular; I'm ready to eat salt junk and sea biscuit. I'll do anything, short of swimming, to get to Singapore by next Wednesday."

"Is it so *very* important?" demanded Captain Blane.

"A wedding. No—no," in answer to his commiserating stare, "not my own—but I've to give away the bride."

"Well, well, I suppose I must try and stretch a point. Mind! I'll take you at your word about the passage money. 'Never refuse a good offer,' is my motto; so, Mr.—?" and he paused interrogatively.

"Lawrence is my name."

"Mr. Lawrence, if you'll be down at Godwin's Wharf to-morrow, at nine o'clock, with your baggage and bedding and servant, we will lie off a bit, and any sampan will put you aboard in five minutes. Ask for the *Wandering Star*;" and with a nod between the clerk and myself, he turned his back and stumped out.

"He is not very keen about passengers, eh?" remarked the clerk with a laugh. "I wonder why?"

"I suppose because she is a dirty old cargo-boat. But any port in a storm, or rather, any ship, in this crisis, for me!"

"Ah," said the clerk, rubbing his chin reflectively, "I've a sort of idea—though perhaps I dreamt it—that there is something rum, or out of the way, about this *Wandering Star*."

"Well, whatever it is, I'll risk it," I answered with a laugh, as I followed the captain's example, and took my departure.

Punctually at nine o'clock next morning I embarked in a sampan, and was rowed down the swift Irrawaddy.

"That cannot be my steamer," I protested, as the boatman made for a long, low, raking craft, a craft of considerable pretensions! She looked like one of the smaller vessels of the P. and O. fleet.

But sure enough the boatman was right, for as we passed under her stern, I read in yellow letters the name— *Wandering Star*.

A closer inspection showed her to be simply what her commander had stated—a tramp; she was dirty, rusty, and travel-stained. When I clambered aboard, I found no snowy decks, or shining brasses, but piles of cargo, bustling coolies, and busy blue-clad lascars. I was immediately accosted by the captain, who presented me to the chief officer, and to a fellow-traveller, a sallow, lanky youth of nineteen, going to join his friends in the Straits.

"I thought he would be company for you," explained the sailor. "We are off in half an hour," pointing to the Blue Peter at the fore. "And we're loaded to the hatches. Mr. Kelly here will show you your quarters."

As I followed the chief officer, I was astonished at the dimensions of the *Star*; it was a considerable distance from the captain's snug cabin, near the bridge, to the poop. We made our way below, into a long saloon with tables and seats intact, but the aft part piled high with bales. There was a strange, musty, mouldy smell; it felt damp and vault-like, and afforded a sharp contrast to the blazing sun and cobalt sky on deck.

As my eye became used to the gloom, I noticed the lavish carving, the handsome mahogany and brass fittings, the maple-wood doors and panels—the remains of better days!

My cabin contained two bunks, and in one of these my servant, a Madras butler, called "Sawmy", had already arranged my bedding.

"I wonder you don't carry passengers?" I remarked to Mr. Kelly. "What a fine saloon! I should have thought it would have paid well."

"She carried hundreds in her day," he said complacently. "You see there is where the piano was hitched, and there the swinging lamps, and bookcase; but, all the same, it would never pay *us* to take passengers;" and he laughed—an odd sort of laugh. "We are not a regular liner, you know, trading between two ports. Regular liners look on us as dirt; but lots of 'em would give a good deal for our lines, and our engines. There's some of them I would not send my old boots home in! We pick up cargo as we find it; one time we run to Zanzibar, another to Hong Kong, another to the Cape, or maybe Sydney. I've not been home this three years. I hope you'll find your bunk comfortable; the youngster is opposite, just across the saloon—you know your way back!" and having done the honours, left me.

Certainly, the *Star* was much above her present business, and bore the remains of having seen better days. Even my marble washstand was not in keeping with a cargo-steamer. I opened the next cabin; it was crammed to the door with freight—bird-cages in this instance. Every cabin was no doubt similarly packed. I was not sorry to exchange the earthy, chill atmosphere below for the bright sunshine on deck. Soon we had weighed anchor, and were moving smoothly down the rapid Irrawaddy, between high banks of tawny grass, gradually losing sight of the shipping, then of the golden Pagoda, then of Elephant Point; finally the *Star* put her nose straight out, to cross the Gulf of Martaban. The sea was calm, we were well fed and found, and made a pleasant party of six; the captain, first and second officers, the chief engineer, and two passengers. I slept like a top that night, and awoke next morning, and found we were anchored off Moulmein, with its hills covered with pagodas and palms. From Moulmein we put to sea, and still the weather once more favoured us. The captain was a capital companion, full of anecdotes and sea-stories; the chief engineer was a first-rate chess-player, and I began to think I had done rather a smart thing in securing a passage in this stray steamer. As the captain concluded a thrilling yarn apropos of a former ship, in which he had been third officer, I suddenly recalled the shipping clerk's hint, and asked—

"Are there no stories about this one? has she no history?"

Captain Blane looked at the chief officer with a knowing grin, and then replied—

"History?—of course she has. What do you call the log-book? That's her history. I suppose that chap at the office told you she was considered an unlucky ship? Eh? Come, now, own up!"

"No; but he said he had an idea that there was something queer about her—he could not remember what it was."

"Well, I've been in command of her now four years, and I've seen nothing to complain of. What do you say, Kelly?" appealing to the first officer.

"I say that I never wish to put foot on a better sea-boat, and there's nothing wrong with her, as far as *I* know."

But Sawmy, my Madras boy, entertained a totally different opinion of the *Star*. When I asked him why he did not sleep outside my door in the saloon, he frankly replied—

"Because plenty devil in this ship; the chief Serang" (head of the Lascars) "telling me that saloon plenty bad place."

19

❀

We were now within forty-eight hours of Singapore, when the weather suddenly changed, as it frequently does in those treacherous seas. The awning was taken down—sure presage of a bad time coming. The ports were closed, and all was made ready for a blow; and we were not disappointed—it came. We had a rough night, but I was not in the least inconvenienced; I slept like a dormouse rocked in the cradle of the deep.

In the morning my fellow-passenger (whose name, by the way, was Mellish, and who had evidently "suffered", to judge by his ghastly appearance) accosted me timidly and said—

"Did you get up and walk about last night?"

"No."

"Do you ever walk in your sleep?" he continued.

"Not to my knowledge—why?"

"Because last night some one came and hammered on my cabin door, and shouted, 'The ship's aground.' What do you think it can have been?" he asked with a frightful face,

"I think there is no doubt that it was the hot tinned lobster you had for supper," I answered promptly.

"No, no, no, it was not a dream—it woke me," he returned. "I thought it was *you*. Then I tried to think it was a nightmare, and had almost brought myself to believe it, and was dropping off to sleep, when a cold, cold wet hand was passed slowly across my face;" and he shuddered violently.

"Lobster!" I repeated emphatically.

"No, no. Oh, Mr. Lawrence, I heard moaning and whispering and praying. I'm afraid to sleep in that cabin alone; may I come and share yours?"

"There is no room," I answered, rather shortly. "The top berth is crammed full of my things."

At breakfast there was a good deal of movement, and now and then a loud splash upon the deck. The captain, who had been tapping the barometer, looked unusually solemn, and said—

"We are in for a bit of dirty weather; unless I'm mistaken, there's a cyclone somewhere about. I don't think we shall do more than touch the edge of it, and this is a stout craft, so you need not be uneasy."

This was vastly reassuring, when the sky to the west changed from a lowering grey to an inky black. The wind rose with a whimper, that increased to a shriek; it lashed the sea with fury, lashed it into enormous waves, and, laden as we were, we began to roll, at first majestically, then heavily, then helplessly. We took in great green seas over the bows, tons of water discharged themselves amidships, and made us stagger and groan, but still through it all the engines thumped doggedly on.

We seized our dinner anyhow; sitting, standing, kneeling, adapting ourselves to the momentary angle of the vessel. It was a miserable evening, wet and cold, and Mellish and I went to bed early.

The dead-lights were down, the hatchway closed behind us; we were entirely cut off from the rest of our shipmates for the night, and the saloon smelt more vault-like than ever. I turned away from Mellish's grey frightened face, and stammering, piteous importunities, shut myself into my cabin, bolted the door, went to bed, and fell asleep. Meanwhile the storm increased to a hurricane, the motion was tremendous. I was flung violently out on the floor, as the *Star* made one awful plunge, and then righted herself. I was, needless to state, now thoroughly awake, and scrambling back into my berth, and clinging to the woodwork with both hands, lay listening to the roaring of the tempest, which rose now and then to a shrill shriek, that had a terribly human sound; my heart beat fast, as my ears assured it that I was not merely listening to the raving of the gale, but actually to the piercing screams of women, and the hoarse shouts of men! Just as I had arrived at this amazing conclusion, the door of the cabin was burst open, and an elderly man, in his shirt-sleeves, was hurled in.

"She's going down," he bawled excitedly, "and the hatches are fast."

I sprang up, and the next lurch shot us both out into the saloon. And what a scene did I behold by three lamps that swung violently to and fro! Their fitful light showed me a large number of half-dressed strangers, in the last extremity of mortal fear; there was the horrible, selfish pushing and struggling of a panic-stricken crowd, fighting their way towards the companion-ladder; the wild frenzied distraction people exhibit when striving to escape from some deadly peril; the tumult, the cries and shrieks of frightened women making frantic appeals for rescue—cries heart-rending to hear.

Besides the dense struggling block at one end of the cabin, battling fiercely for escape, there were various groups, apparently resigned to their impending fate. A family at prayer; two men drinking raw brandy out of tumblers; an ayah beating her head upon the floor, and calling on "Ramasawmy"; an old lady, with a shawl over her head, and a Bible on her knee; a young man and a girl, hand locked in hand, whispering last words; a pale woman, with a sleeping child in her arms. I saw them all. I saw Mellish clinging to the saloon hand-rail, his eyes glazed with horror, and gibbering like an idiot.

The crash of broken crockery, the shrieks of despair, the roaring of the wind, the sullen thundering of the seas overhead, combined to make up the most frightful scene that could possibly be imagined.

Then all at once, a beautiful girl, with long dark hair, streaming over a white gown, rushed out of a cabin, and threw herself upon me, flinging her arms round my neck; she sobbed—"Oh, save me—save me! Don't let me die— don't let me die!"

Her wild agonised face was pressed closely to mine; her frantic clasp round my neck tightened like a band of steel—closer, closer, *closer*. I was choking. I could not move or breathe. She was strangling me, as she shrieked in my ear—

"It is coming now! *This is death!*"

There was one awful lurch, a grinding crash, a sinking sensation, a vice-like grip about my throat—and outer darkness.

❀

I was aroused in broad daylight by Sawmy, who had brought my tea and shaving-water. I was lying on the floor of the saloon, and he was stooping over me, with a frightened expression on his broad, brown countenance.

"At first I thinking master dead!" was his candid announcement. "Me plenty fraiding. Why master lying here and no in bed?" Why indeed!

A plunge of my head into cool water, and a cup of tea, brought me to myself, and then I flung on my dressing-gown, and hurried across the saloon to see what had become of the miserable Mellish.

He was stretched in his berth, with a life-belt beside him, rigid and cold, and in a sort of fit.

With brandy, burnt brown paper, and great difficulty, Sawmy and I brought him round. As soon as he had come to his senses, and realised that he was still in the land of the living, he sat up and turned on me quite ferociously, and said—

"And that's what you call *lobster!*"

23

❋

The weather had moderated considerably, and though I had no great appetite, I was able to appear at breakfast. Mellish was too shattered to join us, and lay in a long chair in the deck-house, sipping beef-tea, and hysterically assuring all inquirers that "he would never again set foot in the saloon—no, he would *much* rather die!"

"I suppose you got knocked about a bit last night?" inquired the captain, with a searching glance.

"Not exactly knocked about; I did not mind *that* so much, but—" and I hesitated.

"But you were disturbed?" he added significantly.

"Yes, very much so; I hope I shall never be disturbed in such a way again."

"Then I take it you've seen them—the former passengers? They are generally aboard, they say, in dirty weather."

"Whatever they were, I trust in God I may never witness such another scene."

"You don't wonder now that we are not free of offering cabin accommodation, eh? Not that I ever saw anything myself."

"But you admit that there *is* something."

"So they say"—nodding his head with a jaunty air.

"And what is the explanation? *What* do they say?" I asked impatiently.

"Just this. The *Wandering Star* was once the *Atalanta*, a fine passenger steamer, and, coming out her last trip, she fell in for the tail of a cyclone, and came to grief off the Laccadives; blown out of her course, engine-fires put out, went on a rock, and sank in ten fathoms; every soul on board went down, except a steward and a fireman, who got off on a hen-coop. It was an awful business—sixty-nine passengers, besides officers and crew. She sank like a stone, no time to get battered to pieces, and so she was right well worth her salvage. A company bought her cheap; she was but little damaged—they raised and sold her. She was intended for the pilgrim traffic, from Bombay to Mecca, and in fact she did make a couple of trips; but somehow she got a bad name; the pilgrims said she was possessed of devils—ha! ha!—and so the owners put her into the wheat and rice and general cargo trade, and we have no complaints. She has been at it these five years, and is, as I take you to witness, a grand sea-boat, and has fine accommodation between decks as well as aft; it's only in real dirty weather that there is anything amiss, and that in the saloon. They say," lowering his voice to a hoarse whisper, "they kept the passengers below, battened down; they got no chance for their lives. It was a mistake; they were all drowned like rats in their holes. Mind you, I've seen nothing, and I'm not a superstitious man."

"Would you sleep in the saloon?" I sternly demanded.

"No; for in a blow *my* place is on the bridge. But I'll not deny that a second officer, who has left us, tried a bunk down there once, out of curiosity, and did not repeat the experiment; he was properly scared;" and the captain chuckled at the recollection.

"I suppose we shall get in to-night?" I remarked, as we paced the deck together.

"Yes, about eleven o'clock. We are doing our twelve knots, dirty-looking old hooker as we are!"

"So much the better," I answered, "for you will not be surprised to hear that I'm not anxious to occupy my berth again."

I am thankful to relate that I slept on land that same night, and was not "disturbed".

❋

I often glance at the shipping lists, to see if there is any news of the *Wandering Star*. I note that she is still tramping the ocean from China to Peru, and I have not the smallest doubt but that, on stormy nights, the saloon is still crowded with the distracted spectres of her former passengers.

If You See Her Face

"I heard a voice across the press,
Of one who called in vain."

– Barrack Room Ballads.

Daniel Gregson, Esq., B.S.C., political agent to the Rajah of Oonomore (a child of seven years of age), and Percy Goring, his junior assistant, were travelling from their own state to attend the great Delhi durbar. Mr. Gregson was a civilian of twenty-five years' standing, short of neck, short of stature, and short of temper. His red face, pale prominent eyes, and fierce bushy brows had gained for him the nick-name of "The Prawn"; but he was also known as a marvellously clever financier, ambitious, shrewd, and prompt in action; and by those who were under him, he was less loved than feared. Young Goring was just twenty-six, and much more eager to discuss good shooting, or a good dance, than the assessment of land, the opium trade, or even acting allowances!

The pair journeyed with due ceremony on the native state line, and in the little Rajah's own gilt and royal carriage. *He* was laid up in the palace with chicken-pock, and had wept sorely because he had been unable to accompany his guide, philosopher, and friend to the grand "Tamasha", to wear his new velvet coat, and all his jewels, and to hear the guns, that would thunder in his honour. Child as he was, he was already keenly sensitive respecting his salute!

Meanwhile the agent and his subordinate got on capitally without him, travelling at the leisurely rate of ten miles an hour, that fine November afternoon, surrounded with tiffin-baskets, cigarettes, ice-boxes, and other luxurious accompaniments. About four o'clock the train came to a sudden standstill—there was no station to account for this, merely a country road, a white gate, and a mud hut. The halt resolved itself into a full stop; Mr. Gregson thrust his red face out of the window, and angrily inquired the reason of the delay.

"Beg your pardon, sir," said the Eurasian guard, "there has been a break on the line—bridge gone—and we can't get forward nohow."

Mr. Gregson glanced out on the prospect—the dusty cactus hedge, the white telegraph posts, the expanse of brownish grass, black goats, and jungle.

"Any village, any dâk bungalow?" demanded the political agent, who might have known better than to ask.

"I'm afraid not, your honour. If your honour will wait here, we will send a messenger to the next station on foot, and tell them to telegraph for another train from the junction. This will arrive at the other side of the break, and take you on about twelve o'clock to-morrow."

"And meanwhile we are to sit here!" cried Mr. Gregson, indignantly. "A pretty state of affairs! I'll send a memo to the railway engineer that will astonish him," he said, turning to Goring. "It's four now, and we shall be here till twelve o'clock to-morrow, if we don't mind. We shall be late for the durbar, and I shall have to wire, 'unavoidably absent'."

"I wonder if there is any sport to be had?" said Goring, descending from the carriage, and stretching his long legs. "Any shooting, any black buck?" looking at the guard interrogatively.

"Ah, that reminds me!" exclaimed Mr. Gregson. The Rajah has a hunting box some-where in these parts—Kori; we can go there for the night."

"Yes, your honour," assented a listener, with profound respect; "but it is four koss from here—a 'Kutcha' road—and a very poor part of the state."

"I vote we stop here," said Goring. "We can shoot a bit, and come back and dine, and sleep in the train. We shall be all right and jolly; twice as comfortable as in some tumble-down old summer-house."

"I shall go to Kori, at any rate," rejoined his superior officer, who resented opposition. "The place is kept up, and I've never seen it. This will be a capital opportunity to inspect it."

"But it's four koss away; and how are we to get our baggage, and bedding, and grub over?"

"Coolies," was the laconic rejoinder. "Get them ready to start at once"—to his head servant, with an imperious wave of his hand.

"There is no way of transport for your majesty," said his obsequious bearer with a deep salaam. "No ponies, not even an ekka—unless the 'Protector of the Poor' would stoop to a country cart?" (Which same is a long rude open basket, between two round wooden wheels, and drawn by a pair of bullocks.)

"I really think it is hardly worth while to move," urged Goring, as he cast a greedy eye in the direction of a promising snipe jheel. "It will be an awful fag, and you know you hate walking!"

"You can please yourself, and stay here," said Mr. Gregson, with immense dignity, who, if he hated walking, liked his own way.

As the whole suite (not to mention the commissariat) were bound to accompany him, Goring was compelled to submit; he dared not run counter to his arbitrary companion, who, rejecting with scorn the lowly vehicle that had been suggested, set out for Kori on foot, whither a long string of coolies had already preceded him. The sandy country road wound over a barren, melancholy-looking tract, diversified with scanty pasture and marshy patches (or jheels), pools of water, tall reeds, and brown grasses. It was dotted with droves of lean cattle, paddy birds, milk-white herons, and cranes—especially the tall sirius family, who danced to one another in a stately, not to say solemn, fashion.

Truly a bleak, desolate-looking region, and, save one or two miserable huts and some thorn bushes, there was no sign of tree or human habitation. At last they came in sight of a wretched village—the once prosperous hanger-on of the now deserted hunting palace—that showed its delicate stone pinnacles behind a high wall; apparently it stood in an enclosure of vast extent, an enclosure that must have cost lakhs of rupees. Two sahibs were naturally an extraordinary sight in this out-of-the-way district; the fame and name of Mr. Gregson, a Burra-Burra sahib, had been spread before him by the coolies, therefore beggars and petitioners swarmed eagerly round this great and all-powerful personage.

Mr. Gregson liked to feel his own importance at a durbar, or an official dinner, but it was quite another matter to have it thrust upon him by a gang of clamouring paupers—the maimed, the halt, the blind—crying out against taxation, imploring alms, and mercy. He was a hard man, with a quick, impatient temper. An aged blind beldame got in his way, and he struck her savagely with his stick. She shrank back with a sharp cry, and Goring, who was ever known as "a sahib with a soft heart", spoke to her and gave her a rupee—a real rupee; it was years since she had felt one!

"Although she is blind, sahib, beware of her," said an officious youth, with his hair in a top-knot. "She has the evil eye!"

"Peace, dog!" she screamed; then to Goring, "I am a lone old woman; my kindred are dead—I have lived too long. I remember the former days—rich days; but bad days. Sahib, if you would be wise, go not to the palace Khana."

Goring was moving on when the hag hastily clutched him by the sleeve, and added in a rasping whisper—

"If you see her face—you die!"

"She is mad," he said to himself, as he hastened to join Mr. Gregson, who had arrived at the great iron-studded gates in a state of crimson fury.

"You say we have land—true!" shouted a haggard, wild-eyed ryot; "but what is land without crops? What is a remission of five per cent to wretches like us? It is but as a caraway seed in a camel's mouth! The wild beasts take our cattle and destroy our grain, and yet we must work and pay you, and starve! Would that the Rajah was a man grown! Would that *you* were dead!"

Mr. Gregson hurried inside, and banged the great gate violently in the face of the importunate crowd.

"It is a very poor district, and much too heavily assessed," said Goring to himself. "There is not even a pony in the place. The very Bunnia is in rags; the deer eat the crops, such as they are, since the deer are preserved, and there is no one now to shoot them. It is abominable!"

The palace was a pretty, light stone building, two stories in height, with a tower at either end, and a double verandah all the way round. In front of it a large space was paved with blocks of white marble, which ran the whole length of the building, and it was surrounded by the most exquisite gardens, kept up in perfect order—doubtless by the taxes wrung from the wretched creatures outside its gates—a garden that was never entered by its proprietor or enjoyed by any one from year's end to year's end, save the mallee's children and the monkeys. The monkeys ate the fruit, the roses and lilies bloomed unseen, the fountains dripped unheeded; it was a paradise for the doves and squirrels, like a garden in a fairy tale.

The chokedar and head mallee (*he* was a rich man) received their great guest with every expression of humble delight. Dinner was prepared with much bustle in the hall of audience, whilst Mr. Gregson and his junior explored. There were long shady walks paved with white marble, immense bushes of heliotrope and myrtle, delicate palms, fine mango trees, peach trees, and orange trees. It was truly an oasis in the desert when one contrasted it with the bare, desolate, barren country that lay outside its walls.

"I shall bring the little chap here," said Mr. Gregson, pompously. "We will have a camp here at Christmas." And then he strolled back to the palace, and made an excellent dinner of roast turkey, and asparagus, and champagne.

After this repast he got out his despatch-box and his cigarette-case, and set about writing an official, whilst Goring took a chair, and adjourned to the marble pavement outside the palace.

It was an exquisite night; a low moon was peering over the wall—the air was heavy with the scent of syringa and orange blossoms; there was not a sound, not a voice to be heard, not a soul in sight, save Mr. Gregson, who, illuminated by two wax candles, bent eagerly over his pen, as he sat in the open hall of audience.

Goring, as he smoked, thought of many things; of the half-famished villagers; of the splendid shooting that was going to waste; of the grand bag he could make, and would make, at Christmas. Then he began sleepily to recall some stories—half-told stories—about this very place; tales of hideous atrocities, and crimes that had been done here, in the days of the Tiger Rajah, the present ruler's grandfather. He was gradually dozing off, when he was aroused by the sounds of distant tom-toms, playing with extravagant spirit. The drumming came slowly nearer and nearer; it actually seemed to be in the garden—louder and louder—with a whispered murmuring and low applause, and as it were the footsteps of a great multitude. But there was nothing whatever to be seen, and it was as light as day. He moved uneasily in his chair, and gazed behind him; no! nothing to be seen but his senior steadily covering sheets of foolscap. He turned his head, and was aware of an unexpected sight—as startling as it was uncanny! Two twinkling little brown feet, dancing before him on the marble pavement! exquisite feet, that seemed scarcely to touch the ground, and that kept perfect time to the inspiriting sounds of the tom-toms; they were decked with massive golden anklets, which tinkled as they moved, and above them waved a few inches of the heavy yellow gold-embroidered skirt of the dancing-girl. No more was visible. Round and round the fairy feet flitted, in a very poetry of motion; faster and faster played the tom-toms. Such dancing, such nimble feet, it had never been young Goring's lot to behold! Yes—but where was the rest of the body?

As he gazed in half-stupefied amazement, he suddenly recalled the old hag's warning, with an unpleasant thrill—

"*If you see her face—you die!*"

At this instant there was a scraping sound, of the pushing back of a chair, of slow footsteps on the marble, of a loud cry, and a heavy fall.

Goring jumped up, and beheld Mr. Gregson lying prone on his face. He rushed to his assistance, and raised him with considerable difficulty. His eyes were fixed with an expression of unutterable horror. He gave one or two shuddering gasps, his head drooped forward on his breast, and he expired.

Goring looked round apprehensively. The feet had disappeared; the tom-toms had ceased.

He shouted for help, and immediately a vast crowd of dismayed retainers assembled around him, and Babel ensued.

"The Burra sahib dead! Well, well, it was ever an evil place. Ah, bah! Ah, bah! It was the nautch-girl, without doubt."

They further informed Goring that the old Rajah had once tortured a dancing-girl on that very spot, and inhumanly disfigured her face. More than one had seen her since, and perished thus.

That morning, at sunrise, the dead body of Mr, Gregson was placed in a native cart, similar to the one he had so scornfully rejected, and taken by slow stages to the nearest station and back to the city, accompanied by Goring.

The doctors, European and native, declared with one consent that Mr. Gregson had died in a fit—an apoplectic seizure.

Goring—wise man—said nothing.

The Red Bungalow

It is a considerable time since my husband's regiment ("The Snapshots") was stationed in Kulu, yet it seems as if it were but yesterday, when I look back on the days we spent in India. As I sit by the fire, or the sunny corner of the garden, sometimes when my eyes are dim with reading I close them upon the outer world, and see, with vivid distinctness, events which happened years ago. Among various mental pictures, there is not one which stands forth with the same weird and lurid effect as the episode of "The Red Bungalow".

Robert was commanding his regiment, and we were established in a pretty spacious house at Kulu, and liked the station. It was a little off the beaten track, healthy and sociable. Memories of John Company and traces of ancient Empires still clung to the neighbourhood. Pig-sticking and rose-growing, Badminton and polo, helped the residents of the place to dispose of the long, long Indian day—never too long for me!

One morning I experienced an agreeable surprise, when, in reading the Gazette, I saw that my cousin, Tom Fellowes, had been appointed Quartermaster-General of the district, and was to take up the billet at once.

Tom had a wife and two dear little children (our nursery was empty), and as soon as I had put down the paper I wired to Netta to congratulate and beg them to come to us immediately. Indian moves are rapid. Within a week our

35

small party had increased to six, Tom, Netta, little Guy, aged four, and Baba, a dark-eyed coquette of nearly two. They also brought with them an invaluable ayah—a Madrassi. She spoke English with a pretty foreign accent, and was entirely devoted to the children.

Netta was a slight young woman with brilliant eyes, jet black hair, and a firm mouth. She was lively, clever, and a capital helpmate for an army man, with marvellous energy, and enviable taste.

Tom, an easy-going individual in private life, was a red-hot soldier. All financial and domestic affairs were left in the hands of his wife, and she managed him and them with conspicuous success.

Before Netta had been with us three days she began, in spite of my protestations, to clamour about "getting a house".

"Why, you have only just arrived," I remonstrated. "You are not even half unpacked. Wait here a few weeks, and make acquaintance with the place and people. It is such a pleasure to me to have you and the children."

"You spoil them—especially Guy!" she answered with a laugh. "The sooner they are removed the better, and, seriously, I want to settle in. I am longing to do up my new house, and make it pretty, and have a garden—a humble imitation of yours—a Badminton court, and a couple of ponies. I'm like a child looking forward to a new toy, for, cooped up in Fort William in Calcutta, I never felt that I had a real home."

"Even so," I answered, "there is plenty of time, and I think you might remain here till after Christmas."

"Christmas!" she screamed. "I shall be having Christmas parties myself, and a tree for the kids; and you, dear Liz, shall come and help me. I want to get into a house next week."

"Then pray don't look to me for any assistance. If you make such a hasty exit the station will think we have quarrelled."

"The station could not be so detestable, and no one could quarrel with *you*, you dear old thing," and as she stooped down and patted my cheek, I realised that she was fully resolved to have her own way.

"I have yards and yards of the most lovely cretonne for cushions, and chairs, and curtains," she continued, "brought out from home, and never yet made up. Your Dirzee is bringing me two men tomorrow. When I was out riding this morning, I went to an auction-room—John Mahomed, they call the man—and inspected some sofas and chairs. Do let us drive there this afternoon on our way to the club, and I also wish to have a look round. I hear that nearly all the good bungalows are occupied."

"Yes, they are," I answered triumphantly. "At present there is not *one* in the place to suit you! I have been running over them with my mind's eye, and either they are near the river, or too small, or—not healthy. After Christmas the Watsons are going home; there will be their bungalow—it is nice and large, and has a capital office, which would suit Tom."

We drove down to John Mahomed's that afternoon, and selected some furniture—Netta exhibiting her usual taste and business capacity. On our way to the club I pointed out several vacant houses, and, among them, the Watsons' charming abode—with its celebrated gardens, beds of brilliant green lucerne, and verandah curtained in yellow roses.

"Oh yes," she admitted, "it is a fine, roomy sort of abode, but I hate a thatched roof—I want one with tiles—red tiles. They make such a nice bit of colour among trees."

"I'm afraid you won't find many tiled roofs in Kulu," I answered; "this will limit you a good deal."

For several mornings, together, we explored bungalows—and I was by no means sorry to find that, in the eyes of Netta, they were all more or less found wanting—too small, too damp, too near the river, too stuffy—and I had made up my mind that the Watsons' residence (despite its thatch) was to be Netta's fate, when one afternoon she hurried in, a little breathless and dusty, and announced, with a wild wave of her sunshade, "I've found it!"

"Where? Do you mean a house?" I exclaimed.

"Yes. What moles we've been! At the back of this, down the next turn, at the cross roads! Most central and suitable. They call it the Red Bungalow."

"The Red Bungalow," I repeated reflectively. I had never cast a thought to it—what is always before one is frequently unnoticed. Also it had been unoccupied ever since we had come to the station, and as entirely overlooked as if it had no existence! I had a sort of recollection that there was some drawback—it was either too large, or too expensive, or too out of repair.

"It is strange that I never mentioned it," I said. "But it has had no tenant for years."

"Unless I am greatly mistaken, it will have one before long," rejoined Netta, with her most definite air. "It looks as if it were just waiting for us—and had been marked 'reserved'."

"Then you have been over it?"

"No, I could not get in, the doors are all bolted, and there seems to be no chokedar. I wandered round the verandahs, and took stock of the size and proportions—it stands in an imposing compound. There are the ruins at the back, mixed up with the remains of a garden—old guava trees, lemon trees, a vine, and a well. There is a capital place at one side for two Badminton courts, and I have mentally laid out a rose-garden in front of the portico."

"How quickly your mind travels!"

"Everything *must* travel quickly in these days," she retorted. "We all have to put on the pace. Just as I was leaving, I met a venerable coolie person, who informed me that John Mahomed had the keys, so I despatched him to bring them at once, and promised a rupee for his trouble. Now do, like a good soul, let us have tea, and start off immediately after to inspect my treasure-trove!"

"I can promise you a cup of tea in five minutes," I replied, "but I am not so certain of your treasure-trove."

"I am. I generally can tell what suits me at first sight. The only thing I am afraid of is the rent. Still, in Tommy's position one must not consider that. He is obliged to live in a suitable style."

"The Watsons' house has often had a staff-tenant. I believe it would answer all your requirements."

"Too near the road, and too near the *General*," she objected, with a gesture of impatience. "Ah, here comes tea at last!"

It came, but before I had time to swallow my second cup, I found myself hustled out of the house by my energetic cousin and *en route* to her wonderful discovery—the Red Bungalow.

We had but a short distance to walk, and, often as I had passed the house, I now gazed at it for the first time with an air of critical interest. In Kulu, for some unexplained reason, this particular bungalow had never counted; it was boycotted—no, that is not the word—*ignored*, as if, like some undesirable character, it had no place in the station's thoughts. Nevertheless, its position was sufficiently prominent—it stood at a point where four ways met. Two gateless entrances opened into different roads, as if determined to obtrude upon public attention. Standing aloof between the approaches was the house—large, red-tiled, and built back in the shape of the letter "T" from an enormous pillared porch, which, with some tall adjacent trees, gave it an air of reserve and dignity.

"The coolie with the keys has not arrived," said Netta, "so I will just take you round and show you its capabilities myself. Here"—as we stumbled over some rough grass—"is where

I should make a couple of Badminton courts, and this"—as we came to the back of the bungalow—"is the garden."

Yes, here were old choked-up stone water-channels, the traces of walks, hoary guava and apricot trees, a stone pergola and a dead vine, also a well, with elaborate tracery, and odd, shapeless mounds of ancient masonry. As we stood we faced the back verandah of the house. To our right hand lay tall cork trees, a wide expanse of compound, and the road; to our left, at a distance, more trees, a high wall, and clustered beneath it the servants' quarters, the cookhouse, and a long range of stables.

It was a fine, important-looking residence, although the stables were almost roofless and the garden and compound a wilderness, given over to stray goats and tame lizards.

"Yes, there is only one thing I am afraid of," exclaimed Netta.

"Snakes?" I suggested. "It looks rather snaky."

"No, the rent; and here comes the key at last," and as she spoke a fat young clerk, on a small yellow pony, trotted quickly under the porch—a voluble person, who wore spotless white garments, and spoke English with much fluency.

"I am abject. Please excuse being so tardy. I could not excavate the key; but at last I got it, and now I will hasten to exhibit premises. First of all, I go and open doors and windows, and call in the atmosphere—ladies kindly excuse." Leaving his tame steed on its honour, the baboo hurried to the back, and presently we heard the grinding of locks, banging of shutters, and grating of bolts. Then the door was flung open and we entered, walked (as is usual) straight into the drawing-room, a fine, lofty, half-circular room, twice as large and well-proportioned as mine. The drawing-room led into an equally excellent dining-room. I saw Netta measuring it with her eye, and she said, "One could easily seat thirty people here, and what a place for a Christmas-tree!"

The dining-room opened into an immense bedroom which gave directly on the back verandah, with a flight of shallow steps leading into the garden.

"The nursery," she whispered; "capital!"

At either side were two other rooms, with bath and dressing-rooms complete. Undoubtedly it was an exceedingly commodious and well-planned house. As we stood once more in the nursery—all the wide doors being open—we could see directly through the bungalow out into the porch, as the three large apartments were *en suite*.

"A draught right through, you see!" she said. "So cool in the hot weather."

Then we returned to the drawing-room, where I noticed that Netta was already arranging the furniture with her mental eye. At last she turned to the baboo and said, "And what is the rent?"

After a moment's palpable hesitation he replied, "Ninety rupees a month. If you take it for some time it will be all put in repair and done up."

"Ninety!" I mentally echoed—and we paid one hundred and forty!

"Does it belong to John Mahomed?" I asked.

"No—to a client."

"Does he live here?"

"No—he lives far away, in another region; we have never seen him."

"How long is it since this was occupied?"

"Oh, a good while—"

"Some years?"

"Perhaps," with a wag of his head.

"Why has it stood empty? Is it unhealthy?" asked Netta.

"Oh no, no. I think it is too majestic, too gigantic for insignificant people. They like something more altogether and *cosy*; it is not cosy—it is suitable to persons like a lady on the General's staff," and he bowed himself to Netta.

I believe she was secretly of his opinion, for already she had assumed the air of the mistress of the house, and said briskly, "Now I wish to see the kitchen, and servants' quarters," and, picking up her dainty skirts, she led the way thither through loose stones and hard yellow grass. As I have a rooted antipathy to dark and uninhabited places, possibly the haunt of snakes and scorpions, I failed to attend her, but, leaving the baboo to continue his duty, turned back into the house alone.

I paced the drawing-room, dining-room, the nursery, and as I stood surveying the long vista of apartments, with the sun pouring into the porch on one hand, and on the green foliage and baked yellow earth of the garden on the other, I confessed to myself that Netta was a miracle!

She, a new arrival, had hit upon this excellent and suitable residence; and a bargain. But, then, she always found bargains; their discovery was her *métier!*

As I stood reflecting thus, gazing absently into the outer glare, a dark and mysterious cloud seemed to fall upon the place, the sun was suddenly obscured, and from the portico came a sharp little gust of wind that gradually increased into a long-drawn wailing cry—surely the cry of some lost soul! What could have put such a hideous idea in my head? But the cry rang in my ears with such piercing distinctness that I felt myself trembling from head to foot; in a second the voice had, as it were, passed forth into the garden and was stifled among the tamarind trees in an agonised wail. I roused myself from a condition of frightful obsession, and endeavoured to summon my common sense and self-command. Here was I, a middle-aged Scotchwoman, standing in this empty bungalow, clutching my garden umbrella, and imagining horrors!

Such thoughts I must keep exclusively to myself, lest I become the laughing-stock of a station with a keen sense of the ridiculous.

Yes, I was an imaginative old goose, but I walked rather quickly back into the porch, and stepped into the open air, with a secret but invincible prejudice against the Red Bungalow. This antipathy was not shared by Netta, who had returned from her quest all animation and satisfaction.

"The stables require repair, and some of the go-downs," she said, "and the whole house must be re-coloured inside, and matted. I will bring my husband round to-morrow morning," she announced, dismissing the baboo. "We will be here at eight o'clock sharp."

By this I knew—and so did the baboo—that the Red Bungalow was let at last!

"Well, what do you think of it?" asked Netta triumphantly, as we were walking home together.

"It is a roomy house," I admitted, "but there is no office for Tom."

"Oh, he has the Brigade Office—Any more objections?"

"A bungalow so long vacant, so entirely over-looked, must have *something* against it—and it is not the rent—"

"Nor is it unhealthy," she argued. "It is quite high, higher than your bungalow—no water near it, and the trees not too close. I can see that you don't like it. Can you give me a good reason?"

"I really wish I could. No, I do not like it—there is something about it that repels me. You know I'm a Highlander, and am sensitive to impressions."

"My dear Liz," and here she came to a dead halt, "you don't mean me to suppose that you think it is haunted? Why, this is the twentieth century!"

"I did not say it was haunted"—(I dared not voice my fears)—"but I declare that I do not like it, and I wish you'd wait; wait only a couple of days, and I'll take you to see the Watsons' bungalow—so sunny, so lived in—always so cheerful, with a lovely garden, and an office for Tom."

"I'm not sure that *that* is an advantage!" she exclaimed with a smile. "It is not always agreeable to have a man on the premises for twenty-four hours out of the twenty-four hours!"

"But the Watsons—"

"My dear Liz, if you say another word about the Watsons' bungalow I shall have a bad attack of the sulks, and go straight to bed!"

It is needless to mention that Tom was delighted with the bungalow selected by his ever-clever little wife, and for the next week our own abode was the resort of tailors, hawkers, butchers, milkmen, furniture-makers, ponies and cows on sale, and troops of servants in quest of places.

Every day Netta went over to the house to inspect, and to give directions, to see how the mallees were laying out the garden and Badminton courts, and the matting people and whitewashers were progressing indoors.

Many hands make light work, and within a week the transformation of the Red Bungalow was astonishing. Within a fortnight it was complete; the stables were again occupied—also the new spick-and-span servants' quarters; Badminton courts were ready to be played upon; the verandah and porch were gay with palms and plants and parrots, and the drawing-room was the admiration of all Kulu. Netta introduced plants in pots—pots actually dressed up in pongee silk!—to the station ladies; her sofa cushions were frilled, she had quantities of pretty pictures and photos, silver knick-knacks, and gay rugs.

But before Netta had had the usual name-board—"Major Fellowes, A.Q.M.G."—attached to the gate piers of the Red Bungalow, there had been some demur and remonstrance. My ayah, an old Madrassi, long in my service, had ventured one day, as she held my hair in her hand, "That new missus never taking the old Red Bungalow?"

"Yes."

"My missus then telling her, *please*, that plenty bad place—oh, so bad! No one living there this many years."

"Why—what is it?"

"I not never knowing, only the one word—*bad*. Oh, my missus! you speak, never letting these pretty little children go there."

"But other people have lived there, Mary—"

Never long—so people telling—the house man paint bungalow all so nice—same like now—they make great bargain—so pleased. One day they go away, away, away, never coming back. Please, please," and she stooped and kissed my hand, "speak that master, tell him—*bad* bungalow."

Of course I pooh-poohed the subject to Mary, who actually wept, good kind creature, and as she did my hair had constantly to dry her eyes on her saree.

And, knowing how futile a word to Tom would prove, I once more attacked Netta. I said, "Netta, I'm sure you think I'm an ignorant, superstitious imbecile, but I believe in presentiments. I have a presentiment, dear, about that Bungalow—*do* give it up to please and, yes, comfort me—"

"What! my beautiful find—the best house in Kulu—my *bargain?*"

"You may find it a dear bargain!"

"Not even to oblige you, dear Liz, can I break off my agreement, and I have really set my heart on your *bête noire*. I am so, so sorry," and she came over and caressed me.

I wonder if Netta in her secret heart suspected that I, the Colonel's wife, might be a little jealous that the new arrival had secured a far more impressive looking abode than her own, and for this mean reason I endeavoured to persuade her to "move on".

However, her mind must have been entirely disabused of this by a lady on whom we were calling, who said:

"Oh, Mrs. Fellowes, have you got a house yet, or will you wait for the Watsons'? Such a—"

"I am already suited," interrupted Netta. "We have found just the thing—not far from my cousin's, too—a fine, roomy, cheerful place, with a huge compound; we are already making the garden."

"Roomy—large compound; near Mrs. Drummond," she repeated with knitted brow. "No—oh, surely you do not mean the Red Bungalow?"

"Yes, that is its name; I am charmed with it, and so lucky to find it."

"No difficulty in finding it, dear Mrs. Fellowes, but I believe the difficulty is in remaining there."

"Do you mean that it's haunted?" enquired Netta with a rather superior air.

"Something of that sort—the natives call it 'the devil's house'. A terrible tragedy happened there long ago—so long ago that it is forgotten; but you will find it almost impossible to keep servants!"

"You are certainly most discouraging, but I hope some day you will come and dine with us, and see how comfortable we are!"

There was a note of challenge in this invitation, and I could see with the traditional "half-eye" that Mrs. Dodd and Mrs. Fellowes would scarcely be bosom friends.

Nor was this the sole warning.

At the club a very old resident, wife of a Government employé, who had spent twenty years in Kulu, came and seated herself by me one morning with the air of a person who desired to fulfil a disagreeable duty.

"I am afraid you will think me presuming, Mrs. Drummond, but I feel that I *ought* to speak. Do you know that the house your cousin has taken is said to be unlucky? The last people only remained a month, though they got it for next to nothing—a mere song."

"Yes, I've heard of these places, and read of them, too," I replied, "but it generally turns out that someone has an interest in keeping it empty; possibly natives live there."

"*Any*where but there!" she exclaimed. "Not a soul will go near it after night-fall—there is not even the usual chokedar—"

"What is it? What is the tale?"

"Something connected with those old mounds of brick-work, and the well. I think a palace or a temple stood on the spot thousands of years ago, when Kulu was a great native city.

"Do try and dissuade your cousin from going there; she will find her mistake sooner or later. I hope you won't think me very officious, but she is young and happy, and has two such dear children, especially the little boy."

Yes, especially the little boy! I was devoted to Guy—my husband, too. We had bought him a pony and a tiny monkey, and were only too glad to keep him and Baba for a few days when their parents took the great step and moved into the Red Bungalow.

In a short time all was in readiness; the big end room made a delightful nursery; the children had also the run of the back verandah and the garden, and were soon completely and happily at home.

An inhabited house seems so different to the same when it stands silent, with closed doors—afar from the sound of voices and footsteps. I could scarcely recognise Netta's new home. It was the centre of half the station gaieties—Badminton parties twice a week, dinners, "Chotah Hazra" gatherings on the great verandah, and rehearsals for a forthcoming play; the pattering of little feet, servants, horses, cows, goats, dogs, parrots, all contributed their share to the general life and stir. I went over to the Bungalow almost daily: I dined, I breakfasted, I had tea, and I never saw anything but the expected and the

47

common-place, yet I failed to eradicate my first instinct, my secret apprehension and aversion. Christmas was over, the parties, dinners and teas were among memories of the past; we were well advanced in the month of February, when Netta, the triumphant, breathed her first complaint. The servants—excellent servants, with long and *bonâ fide* characters—arrived, stayed one week, or perhaps two, and then came and said, "Please I go!"

"None of them remained in the compound at night, except the horsekeepers and an orderly; they retired to more congenial quarters in an adjoining bazaar, and the maddening part was that they would give no definite name or shape to their fears—they spoke of "It" and a "Thing"—a fearsome object, that dwelt within and around the Bungalow.

The children's ayah, a Madras woman, remained loyal and staunch; she laughed at the Bazaar tales and their reciters; and, as her husband was the cook, Netta was fairly independent of the cowardly crew who nightly fled to the Bazaar.

Suddenly the ayah, the treasure, fell ill of fever—the really virulent fever that occasionally seizes on natives of the country, and seems to lick up their very life. As my servants' quarters were more comfortable—and I am something of a nurse—I took the invalid home, and Netta promoted her understudy (a local woman) temporarily into her place. She was a chattering, gay, gaudy creature, that I had never approved, but Netta would not listen to any advice, whether with respect to medicines, servants, or bungalows. Her choice in the latter had undoubtedly turned out well, and she was not a little exultant, and bragged to me that *she* never left it in anyone's power to say, "There—I told you so!"

It was Baba's birthday—she was two—a pretty, healthy child, but for her age backward: beyond "Dadda", "Mam-

48

ma", and "Ayah", she could not say one word. However, as Tom cynically remarked, "she was bound to make up for it by and by!"

It was twelve o'clock on this very warm morning when I took my umbrella and topee and started off to help Netta with her preparations for the afternoon. The chief feature of the entertainment was to be a bran pie.

I found my cousin hard at work when I arrived. In the verandah a great bath-tub full of bran had been placed on a table, and she was draping the said tub with elegant festoons of pink glazed calico—her implement a hammer and tacks—whilst I burrowed into the bran, and there interred the bodies of dolls and cats and horses, and all manner of pleasant surprises. We were making a dreadful litter, and a considerable noise, when suddenly above the hammering I heard a single sharp cry.

"Listen!" I said.

"Oh, Baba is awake—naughty child—and she will disturb her brother," replied the mother, selecting a fresh tack. "The ayah is there. Don't go."

"But it had such an odd, uncanny sound," I protested.

"Dear old Liz! how nervous you are! Baba's scream is something between a whistle of an express and a fog-horn. She has abnormal lung power—and to-day she is restless and upset by her birthday—and her teeth. Your fears—"

Then she stopped abruptly, for a loud, frantic shriek, the shriek of extreme mortal terror, now rose high above her voice, and, throwing the hammer from her, Netta fled into the drawing-room, over-turning chairs in her route, dashed across the drawing-room, and burst into the nursery, from whence came these most appalling cries. There, huddled together, we discovered the two children on the table which stood in the middle of the apartment. Guy had evidently climbed up by a chair, and dragged his sister along with him. It was a beautiful afternoon, the sun streamed in upon them, and the room, as far as we could see, was empty. Yes, but not empty to the trembling little creatures on the table, for with wide, mad eyes they seemed to follow the motion of a something that was creeping round the room close to the wall, and I noticed that their gaze went up and down, as they accompanied its progress with starting pupils and gasping breaths.

"Oh! *what* is it, my darling?" cried Netta, seizing Guy, whilst I snatched at Baba.

He stretched himself stiffly in her arms, and, pointing with a trembling finger to a certain spot, gasped, "Oh, Mummy! look, look, *look!*" and with the last word, which was a shriek of horror, he fell into violent convulsions.

But look as we might, we could see nothing, save the bare matting and the bare wall. What frightful object had made itself visible to these innocent children has never been discovered to the present day.

Little Guy, in spite of superhuman efforts to save him, died of brain fever, unintelligible to the last; the only words we could distinguish among his ravings were, "Look, look, look! Oh, Mummy! look, look, look!" and as for Baba, whatever was seen by her is locked within her lips, for she remains dumb to the present day.

The ayah had nothing to disclose; she could only beat her head upon the ground and scream, and declare that she had just left the children for a moment to speak to the milkman.

But other servants confessed that the ayah had been gossiping in the cook-house for more than half an hour. The sole living creature that had been with the children when "It" had appeared to them, was Guy's little pet monkey, which was subsequently found under the table quite dead.

At first I was afraid that after the shock of Guy's death poor Netta would lose her reason. Of course they all came to us, that same dreadful afternoon, leaving the birthday feast already spread, the bran pie in the verandah, the music on the piano; never had there been such a hasty flight, such a domestic earthquake. We endeavoured to keep the mysterious tragedy to ourselves. Little Guy had brain fever; surely it was natural that relations should be together in their trouble, and I declared that I, being a noted nurse, had bodily carried off the child, who was followed by the whole family.

People talked of "A stroke of the sun", but I believe something of the truth filtered into the Bazaar—where all things are known. Shortly after little Guy's death Netta took Baba home, declaring she would never, never return to India, and Tom applied for and obtained a transfer to another station. He sold off the household furniture, the pretty knick-knacks, the pictures, all that had gone to make Netta's house so attractive, for she could not endure to look on them again. They had been in *that* house. As for the Red Bungalow, it is once more closed, and silent. The squirrels and hoo-poos share the garden, the stables are given over to scorpions, the house to white ants. On application to John Mahomed, anyone desirous of becoming a tenant will certainly find that it is still to be had for a mere song!

The Khitmatgar

"Whence and what art thou, execrable shape?" – Milton.

Perhaps you have seen them more than once on railway platforms in the North-West Provinces. A shabby, squalid, weary-looking group, sitting on their battered baggage, or scrambling in and out of intermediate compartments; I mean Jackson, the photographer, and his belongings. Jackson is not his real name, but it answers the purpose. There are people who will tell you that Jackson is a man of good family, that he once held a commission in a crack cavalry regiment, and that his brother is Lord-Lieutenant of his county, and his nieces are seen at Court balls. Then how comes their kinsman to have fallen to such low estate—if kinsman he be—this seedy-looking, unshorn reprobate, with a collarless flannel shirt, greasy deerstalker, and broken tennis shoes? If you look into his face, who runs may read the answer—Jackson drinks; or his swollen features, inflamed nose, and watery and uncertain eye greatly belie him.

Jackson was a *mauvais sujet* from his youth upwards, if the truth must be confessed. At school he was always in trouble and in debt. At Oxford his scrapes were so prominent that he had more than one narrow escape of being sent down. Who would believe, to look at him *now*, that he had once been a very pretty boy, the youngest and best-looking of a handsome family, and naturally his mother's darling?

Poor woman! whilst she lived she shielded him from duns and dons, and from his father's wrath; she pawned her diamonds and handed over her pin-money to pay his bills; she gave him advice—and he gave her kisses. By the time he had joined his regiment, this reckless youth had lost his best friend, but his bad luck—as *he* termed it—still clung to him and overwhelmed him. His father had a serious interview with his colonel, paid up like a liberal parent, and agreed to his son's exchange into a corps in India. "India may steady him," thought this sanguine old gentleman; but, alas! it had anything but the desired effect. In India the prodigal became more imprudent than ever. Cards, racing, simpkin, soon swallowed up his moderate allowance, and he fell headlong into the hands of the sou-cars—a truly fatal fall! Twenty per cent per month makes horrible ravages in the income of a subaltern, and soon he was hopelessly entangled in debt, and had acquired the disagreeable reputation of being "a man who never paid for anything, and always let others in, when it was a question of rupees". Then his name was whispered in connection with some very shady racing transaction, and finally he was obliged to leave the service, bankrupt alike in honour and credit. His father was dead, his brothers unanimously disowned him, and for twenty years he fell from one grade to another, as he roamed over India from Peshawar to Madras, and Rangoon to Bombay. He had been in turn planter, then planter's clerk, house agent, tonga agent; he had tried touting for a tailoring firm and manufacturing hill jams; and here he was at fifty years of age, with a half-caste wife, a couple of dusky children, and scarcely an anna in his pocket. Undoubtedly he had put the coping-stone on his misfortunes when he took for his bride the pretty, slatternly daughter of a piano-tuner, a girl without education, without energy, and without a penny.

Ten years ago Fernanda Braganza had been a charming creature (with the fleeting beauty of her kind), a sylph in form, with superb dark eyes, fairy-like feet, and a pronounced taste for pink ribbons, patchouli, and pearl-powder. This vision of beauty, who had gushed to Jackson with her soul in her exquisite eyes, and who was not insensible to the honour of marrying a gentleman, was she the selfsame individual as this great fat woman, in carpet slippers, and a bulging tweed ulster, who stood with a sallow, hungry-looking child in either hand? Alas! she was.

The Jacksons had come to try their fortunes at Pani-pore—a small up-country station, where there were two European regiments and half a battery of Artillery—for is not Tommy Atkins ever a generous patron to an inexpensive photographer? The finances of the family were at a very low ebb that February afternoon, as they stood on the platform collecting their belongings, a camera and chemicals, a roll of frowsy bedding, a few cooking things, a couple of boxes, also a couple of grimy servants—in India the poorest have a following, and third-class tickets are cheap. Jackson had a "three-finger" peg at the bar, although there was but little in his pocket, besides a few cards and paper posters, and thus invigorated proceeded to take steps respecting the removal of his family.

Poverty forbade their transit in a couple of ticca gharries, and pride shrank from an ekka; therefore Jackson left his wife in the waiting-room whilst he tramped away in the blinding sun and powdery white dust to see if there was accommodation at the Dâk Bungalow. It proved to be crammed, and he had not yet come down to the Serai, or native halting-place. He was (when sober) a man of some resource. He made his way up to the barracks and asked questions, and heard that the station was in the same condition as the Dâk Bungalow, quite full. Even Fever Hall

and Cholera Villa were occupied, and the only shelter he
could put his head into was the big two-storied bungalow in
the Paiwene road. It had been empty for years; it was to be
had at a nominal rent—say two rupees a week—and there
was no fear of any one disturbing him *there!* It was large
and close to the barracks, but greatly out of repair. With
this useful intelligence, Mr. Jackson rejoined his impatient
circle, and, with their goods in a hand-cart, they started off
for this house of refuge without delay.

Past the native bazaar, past the officers' mess, past the
church, then along a straight wide road, where the crisp
dead leaves crackled underfoot, a road lined with dusty
half-bare trees, whose branches stood out in strong relief
against a hard blue sky, whilst a vast tract of grain country,
covered with green barley and ripe sugar-cane, stretched
away on the right. On the left were a pair of great gaunt gate
piers, leading by a grass-grown approach, to the two-storied
bungalow—an imposing-looking house, that was situated
well back from the highway amid a wilderness of trees, and
rank and rotting vegetation. Distance in this case certainly
had lent enchantment to the view! When the little party
arrived under the wide, dilapidated portico, they found all
the doors closed, the lower windows stuffed with boards,
matting, and even paper in default of glass; weeds and creepers abounded, and there was a dangerous fissure in the front
wall. After knocking and calling for about ten minutes, an
ancient chowkidar appeared, looking half asleep. At first he
thought it was merely a party from the station, wishing, as
was their eccentric custom, "to go over" the haunted house,
the Bhootia Bungalow; but he soon learnt his mistake from
the voluble, shrill-tongued mem-sahib.

This family of shabby Europeans, who had arrived
on foot, with all their belongings in a "*tailer*" from the
station, had actually come to stay, to sleep, to *live* on the

premises! Grumbling to himself, he conducted them up an exceedingly rickety, not to say dangerous, staircase—for the lower rooms were dark and damp—to three or four large and cheerful apartments, opening on a fine verandah. Mrs. Jackson was accustomed to pitching her tent in queer places, and in a very short time she had procured from the bazaar a table, a few chairs, and a couple of charpoys, and furnished two rooms—she had but little to unpack—whilst Kadir Bux, the family slave, vibrated between cooking and chemicals. Meanwhile Mr. Jackson, having washed, shaved, and invested himself in his one linen collar and black alpaca coat, set forth on a tour of inspection, to stick up posters and distribute cards. His wife also made her rounds; the upper rooms were habitable, and the verandah commanded a fine view; it overlooked the park-like but neglected compound, intersected with short cut paths, and which, despite its two grand entrance gates, was now without hedge or paling, and quite open to the road, a road down which not a few ladies and gentlemen in bamboo carts or on ponies were trotting past for their evening airing. Below the suite Mr. Jackson had chosen, were the dismal vault-like rooms, the chowkidar with his charpoy and hukka, and beyond, at the back of the bungalow, the servants' quarters and stables, both roofless. Behind these ruins, stretched an immense overgrown garden (with ancient, dried-up fruit trees, faint traces of walks and water-channels, and a broken fountain and sundial) now abandoned to cattle. On the whole, Mrs. Jackson was pleased with her survey. She had never as yet inhabited such a lordly-looking mansion, and felt more contented than she had done for a long time, especially as Jackson was on his best behaviour—he had no friends in the place, and scarcely any funds.

In a short time Mr. Jackson had acquired both. His good address, his gentlemanly voice, and the whisper of his having once been an officer who had come to grief—who had been unfortunate—went far in a military station. With extraordinary discretion he kept his belongings entirely out of sight; he also kept sober, and consequently received a number of orders for photographs of groups, of bungalows, and of polo ponies. He had the eye of an artist and really knew his business, and although some were startled at the strength of the pegs which he accepted, he had a large and lucrative connection in less than no time, and rupees came flowing in fast. As he and the invaluable Kadir worked together, he talked glibly to portly field-officers and smooth-faced subalterns, of men whom *he* had known, men whose names at least were familiar to them—distinguished veterans, smart soldiers, and even celebrated personages. He attended church, and sang lustily out of a little old Prayer-book, and looked such a picture of devout, decayed gentility, that the tender-hearted ladies pitied him and thought him quite romantic, and hastened to order photographs of all their children, or, children being lacking, dogs. Little did they know that Mr. Jackson's shabby Prayer-book would have been sold for drink years previously, only that he found it an absolutely unmarketable article!

Meanwhile Mrs. Jackson was convinced that she was positively about to be "a lady at last". She purchased frocks for her sallow girls, a dress and boots for herself; she set up a rocking-chair and a cook, and occasionally drove to the bazaar in a "ticca" gharry, where she looked down with splendid dignity on the busy bargaining wives of Tommy Atkins. The chaplain's lady had called upon her, also the barrack-sergeant's wife, who lived in a small bungalow or quarters beyond the garden. She had haughtily snubbed this good woman at first, but subsequently had thawed toward her, for several reasons. Jackson, having been uproariously drunk, and unpleasantly familiar to an officer, had now fallen back on the sergeants' mess for his society, and on private soldiers for his patrons. He was still doing a roaring trade, especially in *cartes-de-visite* at six rupees a dozen. He bragged and talked, and even wept, to his listeners in the barrack-rooms, and in the canteen: listeners who thought him an uncommonly fine fellow, liberal as a lord, flinging his coin right and left. They little guessed the usual sequel, or of how the Jackson family were wont to steal out of a station by rail in the grey dawn of an Indian morning, leaving many poor natives, who had supplied their wants in the shape of bread and meat, coffee, and even clothes, to bewail their too abrupt departure. Jackson was "on the drink", as his wife frankly expressed it, never home before twelve o'clock at night, and then had to be helped upstairs, and Mrs. Jackson found these evenings extremely wearisome. She rarely read, but she did a little crochet and not a little scolding; she slept a good deal; and, as long as her coffee and her curry were well and punctually served, she was fairly content, for she was naturally lethargic and indolent. But still she liked to talk, and here she had no one with whom to exchange a word. She pined for the sound of another female tongue, and accordingly one afternoon she arrayed herself in her new hat with scarlet cock's feathers, also her yellow silk gloves, and with the cook as a body-servant and to carry her umbrella, she sallied forth to return the visit of the barrack-sergeant's wife. She had not far to go—only through the garden and across the road. The barrack-sergeant's wife was knitting outside in her verandah, for the weather was "warming up", when Mrs. Jackson, all-gorgeous in her best garments, loomed upon her vision. Now, Mrs. Clark "had no notion of the wives of drunken photographers giving themselves hairs! And don't go for to tell her as ever that Jackson was a gentleman! A fellow that went reeling home from the canteen every night!" But she dissembled her feel-

ings and stood up rather stiffly, and invited her visitor into
her drawing-room, a small apartment, the walls coloured
grey, furnished with cheap straw chairs, covered in gaudy
cretonne, further embellished by billowy white curtains,
tottering little tables, and a quantity of photographs in
cotton velvet frames—a room of some pretensions, and
Mrs. Clark's pride. Its unexpected grandeur was a blow to
Mrs. Jackson, as was also the appearance of two cups of tea
on a tray, accompanied by a plate of four water-biscuits. It
seemed to her that Mrs. Clark also set up for being quite the
lady, although *her* husband was not a gentleman. The two
matrons talked volubly, as they sipped their tea, of bazaar
prices, cheating hawkers, and the enormities of their servants. "My cook," was continually in Mrs. Jackson's mouth.
They played a fine game of brag, in which Mrs. Jackson,
despite her husband who had been an officer, of her cook,
and of her large house, came off second best!

"I can't think," she said, looking round contemptuously,
"how you can bear to live in these stuffy quarters. I am sure
I couldn't; it would kill me in a week. You should see the
splendid rooms we have; they do say it was once a palace,
and built by a nabob."

"May be so," coolly rejoined her hostess. "I know it was a
mess-house, and after that an officers' chummery, fifteen or
twenty years ago; but no one would live there now, unless
they had *no other* roof to cover them, and came to a place
like a parcel of beggars!"

"Why, what's up with it?" inquired Mrs. Jackson, suddenly
becoming of a dusky puce, even through her pearl-powder.

"Don't you know—and *you* there this two months
and more?"

"Indeed I don't; what is there to know?"

"And haven't you seen him?" demanded Mrs. Clarke, in
a key of intense surprise—"I mean the Khitmatgar?"

59

"I declare I don't know what you are talking about," cried the other, peevishly, "What Khitmatgar?"

"What Khitmatgar? Hark at her! Why, a short, square-shouldered man, in a smart blue coat, with a regimental badge in his turban. He has very sticking-out, curling black whiskers, and a pair of wicked eyes that look as if they could stab you, though he salaams to the ground whenever you meet him."

"I believe I *have* seen him, now you mention it," rejoined Mrs. Jackson; "rather a tidy-looking servant, with, as you say, a bad expression. But bless you! we have such crowds of officers' messengers coming with chits to my husband, I never know who they are! I've seen him now and then, of an evening, I'm sure, though I don't know what brought him, or whose servant he is."

"Servant!" echoed the other. "Why, he is a ghost—the ghost what haunts the bungalow!"

"Ah, now, Mrs. Clark," said her visitor, patronisingly, "you don't tell me you believe such rubbish?"

"Rubbish!" indignantly, "is it? Oh, just you wait and see. Ask old Mr. Soames, the pensioner, as has been here this thirty year—ask any one—and they will all tell you the same story."

"Story, indeed!" cried Mrs. Jackson, with a loud, rude laugh.

"Well, it's a true story, ma'am—but you need not hear it unless you like it."

"Oh, but I should like to hear it very much," her naturally robust curiosity coming to the front. "Please do tell it to me."

"Well, twenty years ago, more or less, some young officers lived in that bungalow, and one of them in a passion killed his Khitmatgar. They say he never meant to do it, but the fellow was awfully cheeky, and he threw a bottle at his head and stretched him dead. It was all hushed up, but that young officer came to a bad end, and the house began to get a bad name—people died there so often; two officers of *delirium tremens*; one cut his throat, another fell over the verandah and broke his neck—and so it stands empty! No one stays a week."

"And why?" demanded the other, boldly. "Lots of people die in houses; they must die somewhere."

"But *not* as they do there!" shrilly interrupted Mrs. Clark. "The Khitmatgar comes round at dusk, or at night, just like an ordinary servant, with pegs or lemonade and so on. Whoever takes anything from his hand seems to get a sort of madness on them, and goes and destroys themselves."

"It's a fine tale, and you tell it very well," said Mrs. Jackson, rising and nodding her red cock's feathers, and her placid, dark, fat face. "There does be such in every station; people must talk, but they won't frighten *me*."

And having issued this manifesto, she gave her hostess a limp shake of the hand and waddled off.

"She's jealous of the grand big house, and fine compound, fit for gentry," said Mrs. Jackson to herself, "and she thinks to get me out of it. Not that she could get in! for she has to live in quarters; and she is just a dog in the manger, and, anyways, it's a made-up story from first to last!"

As she reached her abode, and called *"Qui hai! buttie lao!"* a figure came out from the passage, salaamed respectfully, and, by the light of a two-anna lamp on the staircase, she descried the strange Khitmatgar, whose appearance was perfectly familiar to her—a short, square, surly-looking person. No doubt he was one of Kadir's many friends; the lower rooms were generally overrun with his visitors.

"Send Kadir!" she said imperiously, and went upstairs, and as she spoke the man salaamed again and vanished.

The wife of his bosom had a fine tale to tell Mr. Jackson the next morning, as, with a very shaky hand, he was touching up some plates in his own room.

61

"A Khitmatgar that offers free pegs!" he exclaimed, with a shout of laughter. "Too good to be true. Why, I'd take a whisky and soda from the devil himself—and glad to get it. My mouth is like a lime-kiln at this moment—*Qui hai! whisky-pani do!*"

Many days, warm and sweltering days, rolled on; the hot winds blew the crackling leaves before them, blew great clouds of red dust along the roads, blew ladies up to the hills, and dispersed many of Jackson's patrons. But he did not care; he had made a good many rupees; he had more than one boon-companion, and he drank harder than ever. "Why not?" he demanded; "he had earned the money, and had the best right to spend it." He was earning none now. When customers came, Kadir always informed them the sahib was *sota* (asleep). Yes, sleeping off the effects of the preceding night. Mrs. Jackson was accustomed to this state of affairs, and what she called his "attacks". She rocked herself, fanned herself and dozed, and did a little crochet, whilst the two children played quietly in a back room, with old photographs and bits of cardboard. When her husband did awake, and enjoy a few hours' lucid interval, it was only to recall bills and duns, and flashes of his old life: the cool green park at home, the hunting-field, reviews at Aldershot, his pretty cousin Ethel. Then the chill reality forced itself upon his half-crazy brain. The park was this great, barren, scorched compound, with the hot winds roaring across it; the figure in the verandah was not Ethel in her riding-habit, but Fernanda in carpet slippers and a greasy old dressing-gown. Was this life worth living?

Mrs. Jackson had seen the Khitmatgar several times; once she noticed him looking down at her as she ascended the stairs, once he had appeared in answer to her call, carrying a tray and glasses, but she had boldly waved him away, and said, "Send Kadir; why does he allow strangers to do his work?" There was something far too human about the appearance of the man for her to give a moment's credence to the ghost-story.

One still hot night, a night as bright as day, Mrs. Jackson found the air so oppressive that she could not sleep. She lay tossing from side to side on her charpoy, looking out on the moon-flooded verandah, and listening to the indefatigable brain-fever bird, when suddenly she heard her husband's familiar call, *"Qui hai, peg lao!"* He had been drinking as usual, and had fallen into a sodden sleep in his own room.

After an unusually short interval, steps came up the stairs, shoes were audibly slipped off, and there were sounds of the jingling of a glass and bottle.

The door of Mrs. Jackson's apartment opened into the verandah and stood wide, on account of the intense breathless heat of that Indian night. In a few moments some one came and paused on the threshold, tray in hand, some one who surveyed her with a grin of Satanic satisfaction. It was the strange Khitmatgar! There was a triumphant expression in his eyes that made her blood run cold, and whilst she gazed, transfixed with horror, he salaamed and was gone. In a second she had jumped out of bed; she ran into the verandah. Yes, the long verandah was empty—he had disappeared. She called excitedly to her husband; no answer. She rushed into his room, to unfold her experience. Jackson was sitting at the table, or rather half lying across it, his hands clenched, his features convulsed, his eyes fixed—quite dead.

He had swallowed one of his chemicals, a fatal poison. Of course, there was the usual ephemeral excitement occasioned by a tragedy in the station, the usual inquest and verdict of temporary insanity, and then a new nameless grave in the corner of the cantonment cemetery.

❊

Jackson's fate was generally attributed to whisky—or filthy country liquor. "Poor fellow! his position preyed on his mind, and he drank himself to death."

This was the universal opinion in mess-room, barrack-room, and bazaar. But there were one or two people, including his wife and Mrs. Clark, who thought otherwise, and who gravely shook their heads and whispered—*"The Khitmatgar"*.

Her Last Wishes

"Rest, rest, perturbed spirit" – Hamlet.

The Rev. Eustace Herbert was one of the most indefatigable labourers among the poor of a densely crowded parish in the East of London. Slumming with him was not a mere transient caprice, the fashion of a season, a novel page for idle fingers to scan and turn over—it was his life's work, and an inexorable and ever-present duty. His energy was tireless, his zeal inexhaustible, they laid upon his weak, mortal frame more than it could support. Long hours of work and struggle, short hours of sleep, and scanty meals—all these had their due effect on mind and body, and both succumbed. The active, eloquent, indomitable priest emerged from a fever a shattered wreck—a prey to depression, insomnia, and delusions.

He was ordered away to new climes and countries; commanded to forget misery, squalor, crime, cruelty; to cease to puzzle over social problems, and to exchange grey days and grim scenes for mental idleness and golden sunshine.

A sea voyage restored sleep and appetite to the invalid; fresh characters and gay surroundings thrust shabby old tenants from his thoughts, and when he landed in Calcutta the Rev. Eustace Herbert was already a new man!

He travelled much and far, and was confronted on every side by old religions and shameless, gaudy idolatry. He beheld with amazed eyes the stern piety of the Mahomedans;

their prompt answers to summons to prayer. He listened to the sonorous eloquence of a turbaned missionary, preaching the Prophet, at the corner of the street. Religion was an all-important ingredient in daily life, its observance a matter of course, in this vast heathen land! The fact was unpleasantly brought home to him when his hired coachman suddenly dropped from his box, at sundown, and, leaving his horses (a splendid instance of simple faith), prostrated himself on his face in a public thoroughfare.

What would a Londoner think (or say) if his driver were to behave in a like manner? The great pilgrimages were another revelation to the stranger—the fierce, unshaken belief of thousands, as testified by their toil- some journeys and incredible hardships.

The young priest measured with envious eyes the vast multitude which blackened the banks of the Ganges, and recalled with a glow of shame the dimensions of his own scanty flock, whose attendance was often due to a carnal desire for further donations of port wine, beef tea, and fuel.

He penetrated south—to old Madras, to out-of-the-world, teeming cities—fastnesses of Brahminism—on which one glimmer of nineteenth-century thought has never shed a ray! Here he witnessed, as a man in a dream, many curious ceremonies—the sacrifice in high places of sheep and oxen (precisely as in the days of Moses), and half-maddened wretches gashing themselves with knives, like the priests of Baal—and even beheld at a great distance that revolting spectacle known as "hook swinging". Truly, he had many awakening experiences, not the least of which occurred on the platform of Pothanore Railway Station. Here he was suddenly accosted by a fair, long-haired European, in native dress (turban and dothi all complete), who thrust a copy of the *War Cry* into his astonished hands, and eagerly demanded if he was "saved".

This, as well as every other incident, the Rev. Herbert Eustace carefully inscribed in a large Letts's diary, which he wrote up conscientiously before retiring for the night. All his experiences were entered, with one notable exception—an experience he did not venture to set down in black and white, lest it should be read by unbelievers, discredited, and mocked at! It therefore falls to another to repair the omission, and to record the Rev. Eustace Herbert's curious adventure on the Glenvale Coffee Estate in Mysore.

During his ramblings in the Madras Presidency, the clerical explorer found himself within easy reach—that is to say, within a hundred miles—of the home of an old school-fellow, who had failed for the army, married beneath him, and settled down in India for life.

Mr. St. Maur had heard of his friend's arrival in the country, and had urged him to pay him a visit, in the following terms:—

Glenvale, *via* Oonoor, Mysore.

Dear Eustace,

I understand that you are globetrotting, for your health.

One of our planters heard you preach at Trichinopoly last Sunday—I am glad you don't exceed fifteen minutes—and told me of your whereabouts. You must come and pay me a visit; we are only forty miles from Oonoor Station, where I will meet you. It is whispered that you are writing a book of travels. If so, it is your bounden duty to see everything, including an old worn-out coffee estate, and you may put us all in print, if you choose!

Bar jokes, I will take no refusal, old fellow. I want to see a familiar face from home, to talk over Winchester days, and to get you to christen our son and heir. We have no padre in these regions, and there are several little jobs for you in the way of joining couples together in holy matrimony.

I have been five years on the Glenvale coffee plantation, and am rubbing along fairly well, considering the awful state of the rupee, and one or two wretched seasons. I bought the property for a mere song. It was said to be worked out, and the owners were sick of it and this remote part of the earth. However, I find that some pickings are still to be had. A cheap, healthy, outdoor life suits me. I am my own master, though a married man, and I get some first-class shooting, and have several capital fellow planters in the neighbourhood. I can promise you a hearty welcome, a comfortable room, and the best coffee you ever tasted!

Give me two days' notice, and you will be met at Oonoor Station by your old friend,

J. St. John St. Maur.

Ten days after the receipt of this epistle, the Rev. Eustace Herbert alighted from the train, about sunrise, at an insignificant little platform, with an enormous name board, on which huge English and Tamil characters contended for space. A stalwart Englishman, whose eager eyes looked out between a mushroom topee and a monstrous beard, welcomed the new arrival with a blow on the back that nearly landed that frail person in the middle of the track. A tonga and pair of peevish, wiry ponies were in waiting, and as soon as the conveyance had been loaded up with parcels, boxes, stores of sorts, and Mr. Herbert's modest luggage, he and his host started off, clattering down a steep village street, and away towards the foot of the adjacent Blue Mountains. The road was fair—the "tats" travelled rapidly, by open plain, then dense forest jungle, by rising winding ways, through luxurious tropical scenery, leaving gradually behind them palms, banana-trees, cacti, and sweltering little mud hamlets. On, on, to higher latitudes and colder air—on, up among the coffee and the tea—meeting only lumbering, laden bullock carts, drowsily descending to the low country.

During his forty mile drive the Rev. Eustace Herbert found ample employment for eyes, ears, and tongue. He had much to hear, and yet more to tell.

There was a relay of fresh ponies half-way, and the journey was almost accomplished ere it seemed well begun, so pleasantly had the time—and the miles—flashed by.

The steep, wooded, winding ghaut road had been exchanged for the open plateau, where bright-green downs, dark-green coffee bushes, and the delicate tea plant, divided the soil.

"Here we are on the Glenvale Estate, at last," said St. Maur, as they turned down a by-road to the left. "There is the bungalow—it faces due south; we approach it at the back, as you see."

"It's a big place!" remarked his guest, "like an English country house."

"Yes, it is big—too big for us. It was built fifty years ago, when people did things on a large scale, and lived out in India all their lives. The Mortons owned miles up here—labour was cheap, coffee was dear; they made their pile—at least, old Morton did; the property was divided and split up. I bought this bit with the house—I got it dirt cheap, from a chap called Fleming; he only stayed here a couple of years—he could not stand the life, and bolted."

"It looks a most delightful retreat," cried his friend, as they rapidly drew near a great stone, flat-roofed bungalow, with a deep pillared verandah, embowered in passion flowers. It was not engulfed to the very steps in coffee bushes, like many a planter's house, but haughtily held the business, plant, and premises, at a distance, and was surrounded by at least twenty acres of short grass, dotted with cinchona trees and clumps of firs. A well-kept avenue wound up to the verandah; there was no particular hall door, but a dumpy, little woman, in a washed-out print gown, stood on the steps to receive them. This was Mrs. St. John St. Maur—late Miss Jane Bodd, factory hand, of Lancashire, England—who awkwardly welcomed her guest in an exceedingly broad provincial dialect. Yes, and she was fat, freckled, and ordinary. What had possessed St. Maur! thought his schoolfellow. His wife must have some brilliant qualities, to atone for such lamentable deficiencies—in grace, manners, beauty, and fortune. (She was a cheerful, even-tempered person, a notable housekeeper—this in the jungle is a valuable accomplishment, and covers a multitude of shortcomings.)

"Joe, did you bring the bacon?" she demanded breathlessly. "Did ye find all the things at the station?"

"Yes; all but the books from Higginbotham."

"Ah, well, them's no matter; but we couldn't well want the lamp oil, and beer, and champagne. Come in, Mr. Herbert; come in do, ye must be starving. Joe here will show you your room, and tiffin is just ready."

"My wife is not literary," explained St. Maur with a smile. "You won't find any yellow asters, lilac sun bonnets, or green carnations lying about our diggings, but she will make you comfortable. Now tell me, what do you think of this?" and he flung wide a door.

His companion uttered an involuntary exclamation of surprise, the immense room which he entered opened straight into a wide verandah that overlooked the most exquisite prospect his eyes had ever rested upon.

A long valley, sloping away to the misty blue plains, and bounded on either hand by majestic purple mountains; the immediate foreground was filled by a flower garden laid out in true old English fashion, with neat box borders, and gravelled paths, blooming with luxuriant rose bushes, myrtles, heliotropes, gigantic fuchsias, and fragrant orange-trees. A shallow flight of stone steps led from it to a gentle descent of greensward, a kind of wild pleasure ground, with clumps of rhododendrons, acacias, and oaks. This, in turn, gradually lost itself in the surrounding jungle of boulder stones, forest trees, and tree ferns.

The sweet scent of flowers, the balmy afternoon air, penetrated the spare room, which was spacious, lofty, and scrupulously neat; it was, moreover, unexpectedly luxurious, being furnished with handsome, old, carved, black wood furniture—a bed, bureau, wardrobe, and toilet-table. The floor was covered with a thick but faded Indian carpet, and the huge rosewood cheval-glass and velvet couch claimed the visitor's respect.

"I took over the bungalow, lock, stock, and barrel," explained St. Maur. "This room is just as it stood in old Morton's time; it was his daughter's, I believe, and that was her garden. I hope you will find it comfortable."

To this query the Reverend Eustace gave an enthusiastic assent; this guest chamber, with its windows opening into a lovely pleasure-ground, and commanding an unsurpassed view, was a room in which to entertain happy or noble thoughts, and to dream enchanting dreams. The visitor was charmed with everything he was introduced to—from the quaint old bungalow, with its air of age and better days, to the great white pulping-house and the small red baby.

Worn out by his journey, and soothed by the perfume-laden air, the Rev. Eustace Herbert fell asleep almost as soon as he laid his head on the pillow. It was a full moon that sailed in the sky, and her light was as bright as day. One of the windows stood wide open that warm April night; gradually the traveller's eyes closed on his surroundings, on the shrubs in the garden, throwing sharp black shadows on the vague objects in the room—on the whole world. He slept profoundly for some time, when all at once, and for no apparent reason, he found himself distinctly wide awake! It seemed to him that he heard a faint, but distinctly audible, sigh. Surely there was some one in the room?

Yes. A woman in a white gown was sitting at the dressing-table, leaning her head on her hand. He raised himself stealthily on his elbow, and saw that she was absorbed in a volume which lay open before her. It was his own Prayer-book. Presently he sat up, and gave a gentle cough of expostulation.

The lady slowly turned her head, and looked at him. She had a pair of deep pathetic eyes, and a pretty young face—but it was wan and sad.

Then she rose wearily, as if she was extremely tired, passed through the open window, and walked out into the garden without sound of footfall. Who could she be?—he had not seen her the previous evening. He jumped from his bed, rushed to the verandah, and gazed up and down—there was no one within sight. Then he glanced at his open Prayer-book, and gave a violent and involuntary start, for it lay wide open at "The Service for the Burial of the Dead".

The next morning her visitor discovered Mrs. St. Maur bustling about among her stores and servants—excessively busy with preparations for the christening, and two weddings, which were to take place that same afternoon.

She, however, found time, between voluble orders in the Tamil language, to ask him how he had slept, and she eyed him a little anxiously.

"Like a top, thank you."

"That's all right"—turning away.

"But," he added, "every one else is not so fortunate."

Mrs. St. Maur paused, and stared.

"Surely you have a somnambulist on the premises. Have you not?"

"Laws—no! I never heard of that sort of religion—but my cook says he is a Baptist!"

"Oh, I don't mean that—but some one who walks in their sleep, don't you know?"

Mrs. St. Maur gaped at him open-mouthed.

"I never heard of the like—no one walks here! Happen you'd a nightmare—we had pork for dinner. You think some one was tramping round?"

"Yes, I am sure of it."

"It might have been the chokedar. Last time young Forbes slept in that room, he complained of him, and said he saw him poking about the dressing-table. I did give it to the old gentleman, though he declared he never was that side of the house all night."

As the Reverend Eustace turned to greet her husband, he distinctly heard her mutter to herself, in a querulous aside, "There's always complaints about that room."

The christening and the two weddings (one of a planter's assistant, and the other of a Eurasian clerk) took place at Glenvale, with great éclat. There was a cake from D'Angelis, champagne, quantities of real orange blossoms, and a large and merry company who had assembled from all the surrounding estates, in order to make holiday.

73

By ten o'clock, however, the last tonga, the last lazy bullock bandy, and the last reluctant pony, had departed, and peace, silence, and moonlight once more fell upon the Glenvale estate.

And once more towards the small hours, the reverend guest was aroused, and again he saw the lady reading at his dressing-table, a young lady, who raised her head and gazed at him with eyes of haggard reproach, then arose deliberately, sauntered through the open window, passed down the garden towards the slope, and with a quick, beckoning wave of her hand, disappeared amidst a clump of far-distant rhododendrons. Yes. There was the Prayer-book wide open in the same place; the whole occurrence was exceedingly mysterious. There was no use in questioning Mrs. St. Maur, but over a morning pipe in the verandah he unfolded his experience to her husband.

"At first I thought it was one of my old delusions, but my head is clear enough, and I never was better in my life. What does it mean, Joe? Can you explain it in any reasonable way?"

"No; but perhaps old Murphy, who was overseer here for twenty years, can throw some light on it. He was born and bred on these hills and lived with his daughter in Co-imbatore. He happens to be up now, with his son, who has a small tea estate, the other side of the ghaut. He is coming round this afternoon, I know, to drink the kid's health, and look at the new crop. If any one can tell us yarns about this place, he can, and he will be willing enough—for he is the greatest talker in the Presidency. You say you distinctly saw the girl pass through the garden, down the slope, and then turn and beckon to you before she disappeared among the trees? I must confess that I wonder you did not follow her."

"Yes—but I was in my sleeping suit and bare feet, you see, and I must confess that I never had the least impulse to do so; quite the contrary, in fact."

"Suppose we go and make a search now; you can tell me the bearings of whereabouts she vanished?"

"Of course I can; it was quite a long way down—near a rhododendron clump. Come on."

The two old schoolfellows turned off to the slope, and to where it was bounded by the greedy, ever insatiable jungle. They pushed aside some straggling branches of a great overgrown rhododendron, and there discovered a long, significant mound—in short, a grave. As they stood looking at one another across it, a loud hearty voice exclaimed:

"So you have it at last! I always knew it would be found some day—I mean where Miss Nellie Morton was buried!"

"Hullo, Murphy, is that yourself?" cried St. Maur. "Glad to see you. Who was Miss Nellie Morton, and why was she buried here?"

"She was buried here because she died here, of cholera, poor dear child! and she was young Morton's only sister. She lived with him and his wife. The black cholera was raging round, and the coolies, and servants, and every living soul, fled the place—just ran for their dear lives—never stopped to pack a bundle, or to turn a key. It was awful bad in these hills, that season! Miss Nellie got it from nursing her ayah— she was took herself in a couple of hours. Young Morton and one of his assistants buried her—no one knew when or where—and then he and his wife cleared out that same hour; but he and his assistant got cholera too, and died on their way down the Seegor Ghaut; you may see the graves by the roadside any day. His wife never came back here; she always hated the place, for she was main fond of balls and society, and used to sit crying, for amusement and company, for hours together! But Miss Nellie, she loved every inch and stone of Glenvale. You see, she was born here, but eddicated at home; she knew every path for miles. It was she made the flower garden and the seat under the orange tree, and she was a great horsewoman, and a real beauty too. Young Norris, across the valley, was her intended husband, and he was away in Madras on business; and when he came back again here, and found the whole place deserted, the cattle and fowl straying wild, and her dead, he nearly went mad, and no wonder. He could never find her grave—not though he searched for days and days—and no one knew where she was laid by her brother, seeing as he was gone too; but you discovered it easily enough, sir"—nodding at the clergyman.

"Yes," he replied, with a meaning look at his friend; "I had no difficulty at all."

"Mr. Norris is not young Norris now, but he has never married—he lives alone across the valley, and I am sure he would be very thankful to know where she lies—at long last."

"Yes," assented St. Maur, "we will send him word, but the news need not be given out elsewhere. Don't tell Janie"—addressing his guest; "she is awfully superstitious. She would not stay here an hour if she suspected that there was a ghost in the house. I knew that the bungalow stood empty for years before Fleming came, and I did hear that the reason he cleared out was that he could not stand a girl who came and cried and beckoned to him at the door; but as I knew he had had D.T. several times, and made the same complaints of sheep, and cockatoos, and snakes, I thought nothing of it. However, I now remember that one or two planter fellows said they could never sleep properly in that room; it was too big, so they declared—but the truth is, I suppose, they were ashamed to confess that they had seen her!"

That same evening the christening and wedding ceremonies were supplemented by another, which was held privately at sundown—over the grave among the rhododendrons. Only Mr. Norris, Old Murphy, Mr. St. Maur, and his friend were present. And it is an unquestionable fact that, after this service, the figure in the spare room was never seen again.

The Rev. Eustace Herbert duly published his book, *Six Months among Strange Sights*: it has appeared in neat six-shilling form, but its pages may be searched in vain for the most thrilling of his experiences—the fact that he had complied with an unspoken request from an apparition in the Glenvale guest-chamber, and had personally carried out the last wishes of a ghost!

The Dâk Bungalow at Dakor

"When shall these phantoms flicker away,
Like the smoke of the guns on the wind-swept hill;
Like the Bounds and colours of yesterday,
And the soul have rest, and the air be still?"

– Sir A. Lyall.

"And so you two young women are going off on a three days' journey, all by yourselves, in a bullock tonga, to spend Christmas with your husbands in the jungle?"

The speaker was Mrs. Duff, the wife of our deputy commissioner, and the two enterprising young women were Mrs. Goodchild, the wife of the police officer of the district, and myself, wife of the forest officer. We were the only ladies in Karwassa, a little up-country station, more than a hundred miles from the line of rail. Karwassa was a pretty place, an oasis of civilisation, amid leagues and leagues of surrounding forest and jungle; it boasted a post-office, public gardens (with tennis courts), a tiny church, a few well-kept shady roads, and half a dozen thatched bungalows, surrounded by luxuriant gardens. In the hot weather all the community were at home, under the shelter of their own roof-trees and punkahs, and within reach of ice—for we actually boasted an ice machine! During these hot months we had, so to speak, our "season". The

78

deputy commissioner, forest officer, police officer, doctor, and engineer were all "in", and our gaieties took the form of tennis at daybreak, moonlight picnics, whist-parties, little dinners, and now and then a beat for tiger, on which occasions we ladies were safely roosted in trustworthy trees.

It is whispered that in small and isolated stations the fair sex are either mortal enemies or bosom-friends! I am proud to be in a position to state that we ladies of Karwassa came under the latter head. Mrs. Goodchild and I were especially intimate; we were nearly the same age, we were young, we had been married in the same year and tasted our first experiences of India together. We lent each other books, we read each other our home letters, helped to compose one another's dirzee-made costumes, and poured little confidences into one another's ears. We had made numerous joint excursions in the cold season, had been out in the same camp for a month at a time, and when our husbands were in a malarious or uncivilised district, had journeyed on horseback or in a bullock tonga and joined them at some accessible spot, in the regions of dâk bungalows and bazaar fowl.

Mrs. Duff, stout, elderly, and averse to locomotion, contented herself with her comfortable bungalow at Karwassa, her weekly budget of letters from her numerous olive-branches in England, and with adventures and thrilling experiences at secondhand.

"And so you are off to-morrow," she continued, addressing herself to Mrs. Goodchild. "I suppose you know where you are going?"

"Yes," returned my companion promptly, unfolding a piece of foolscap as she spoke; "I had a letter from Frank this morning, and he has enclosed a plan copied from the D.P.W. map. We go straight along the trunk road for two days, stopping at Korai bungalow the first night and Kular the second, you see; then we turn off to the left on the Old Jubbulpore Road and make a march of twenty-five miles, halting at a place called Chanda. Frank and Mr. Loyd will meet us there on Christmas Day."

"Chanda—Chanda," repeated Mrs. Duff, with her hand to her head. "Isn't there some queer story about a bungalow near there—that is unhealthy—or haunted—or something?"

Julia Goodchild and I glanced at one another significantly. Mrs. Duff had set her face against our expedition all along; she wanted us to remain in the station and spend Christmas with her, instead of going this wild-goose chase into a part of the district we had never been in before. She assured us that we would be short of bullocks, and would probably have to walk miles; she had harangued us on the subject of fever and cholera and bad water, had warned us solemnly against dacoits, and now she was hinting at ghosts.

"Frank says that the travellers' bungalows after we leave the main road are not in very good repair—the road is so little used now that the new railway line comes within twenty miles; but he says that the one at Chanda is very decent, and we will push on there," returned Julia, firmly. Julia was nothing if not firm; she particularly prided herself on never swerving from any fixed resolution or plan. "We take my bullock tonga, and Mr. Loyd's peon Abdul, who is a treasure, as you know; he can cook, interpret, forage for provisions, and drive bullocks if the worst comes to the worst."

"And what about bullocks for three days' journey—a hundred miles if it's a yard?" inquired Mrs. Duff, sarcastically.

"Oh, the bazaar master has sent on a chuprassie and five natives, and we shall find a pair every five miles at the usual stages. As to food, we are taking tea, bread, plenty of tinned stores, and the plum-pudding. We shall have a capital outing, I assure you, and I only wish we could have persuaded you into coming with us."

"Thank you, my dear," said Mrs. Duff, with a patronising smile. "I'm too old, and I *hope* too sensible to take a trip of a hundred miles in a bullock tonga, risking fever and dacoits and dâk bungalows full of bandicoots, just for the sentimental pleasure of eating a pudding with my husband. However, you are both young and hardy and full of spirits, and I wish you a happy Christmas, a speedy journey and safe return. Mind you take plenty of quinine—and a revolver"; and, with this cheerful parting suggestion, she conducted us into the front verandah and dismissed us each with a kiss, that was at once a remonstrance and a valediction.

Behold us the next morning, at sunrise, jogging off, behind a pair of big white bullocks, in the highest spirits. In the front seat of the tonga we had stowed a well-filled tiffin basket, two Gladstone bags, our blankets and pillows, a hamper of provisions, and last, not least, Abdul. Julia and I and Julia's dog "Boss" occupied the back seat, and as we rumbled past Mrs. Duff's bungalow, with its still silent compound and closed venetians, we mutually agreed that she was "a silly old thing", that she would have far more enjoyment of life if she was as enterprising as we were.

Our first day's journey went off without a hitch. Fresh and well-behaved cattle punctually awaited us at every stage. The country we passed through was picturesque and well wooded; doves, peacocks, and squirrels enlivened the roads; big black-faced monkeys peered at us from amid the crops that they were ravaging within a stone's throw of our route. The haunt of a well-known man-eating tiger was impressively pointed out to us by our cicerone Abdul—this beast resided in some dense jungle that was unpleasantly close to human traffic. Morning and afternoon wore away speedily, and at sundown we found ourselves in front of the very neat travellers' bungalow at Korai. The interior was scrupulously clean, and contained the usual furniture:

two beds, two tables, four chairs, lamps, baths, a motley collection of teacups and plates, and last, not least, the framed rules of the establishment and visitors' book. The khansamah cooked us an excellent dinner (for a travellers' bungalow), and, tired out we soon went to bed and slept the sleep of the just. The second day was the same as the first—highly successful in every respect.

On the third morning we left the great highway and turned to the left, on to what was called the Old Jubbulpore Road, and here our troubles commenced! Bullocks were bad, lame, small, or unbroken; one of Mrs. Duff's dismal prophecies came to pass, for after enduring bullocks who lay down, who kicked and ran off the road into their owners' houses, or rushed violently down steep places, we arrived at one stage where there were no bullocks *at all!* It was four o'clock, and we were still sixteen miles from Chanda. After a consultation, Julia and I agreed to walk on to the next stage or village, leaving Abdul to draw the neighbourhood for a pair of cattle and then to overtake us at express speed.

"No one coming much this road now, mem sahib," he explained apologetically; "village people never keeping tonga bullocks—only plough bullocks, and plenty bobbery."

"Bobbery or not, get them," said Julia with much decision; "no matter if you pay four times the usual fare. We shall expect you to overtake us in half an hour." And having issued this edict we walked on, leaving Abdul, a bullock-man, and two villagers all talking together and yelling at one another at the top of their voices.

Our road was dry and sandy, and lay through a perfectly flat country. It was lined here and there by rows of graceful trees, covered with wreaths of yellow flowers; now and then it was bordered by a rude thorn hedge, inside of which waved a golden field of ripe jawarri; in distant dips in the landscape we beheld noble topes of forest trees and a few red-roofed dwellings—the abodes of the tillers of the soil; but, on the whole, the country was silent and lonely; the few people we encountered driving their primitive little carts stared hard at us in utter stupefaction, as well they might—two mem sahibs trudging along, with no escort except a panting white dog. The insolent crows and lazy blue buffaloes all gazed at us in undisguised amazement as we wended our way through this monotonous and melancholy scene. One milestone was passed and then another, and yet another, and still no sign of Abdul, much less the tonga. At length we came in sight of a large village that stretched in a ragged way at either side of the road. There were the usual little mud hovels, shops displaying, say, two bunches of plantains and a few handfuls of grain, the usual collection of gaunt red pariah dogs, naked children, and unearthly-looking cats and poultry.

Julia and I halted afar off under a tree, preferring to wait for Abdul to chaperon us, ere we ran the gauntlet of the village streets. Time was getting on, the sun was setting; men were returning from the fields, driving bony bullocks before them; women were returning from the well, with water and the last bit of scandal; at last, to our great relief, we beheld Abdul approaching with the tonga, and our spirits rose, for we had begun to ask one another if we were to spend the night sitting on a stone under a tamarind tree without the village.

"No bullocks," was Abdul's explanation. The same tired pair had come on most reluctantly, and in this village of cats and cocks and hens it was the same story—"no bullocks". Abdul brought us this heavy and unexpected intelligence after a long and animated interview with the head man of the place.

"What is to be done?" we demanded in a breath.

"Stop here all night; going on to-morrow."

"Stop where?" we almost screamed.

"Over there," rejoined Abdul, pointing to a grove of trees at some little distance. "There is a travellers' bungalow; Chanda is twelve miles off."

A travellers' bungalow! Sure enough there was a building of some kind beyond the bamboos, and we lost no time in getting into the tonga and having ourselves driven in that direction. As we passed the village street, many came out and stared, and one old woman shook her hand in a warning manner, and called out something in a shrill cracked voice.

An avenue of feathery bamboos led to our destination, which proved to be the usual travellers' rest-house, with white walls, red roof, and roomy verandah; but when we came closer, we discovered that the drive was as grass-grown as a field; jungle grew up to the back of the house, heavy wooden shutters closed all the windows, and the door was locked. There was a forlorn, desolate, dismal appearance about the place; it looked as if it had not been visited for years. In answer to our shouts and calls no one appeared; but, as we were fully resolved to spend the night there, we had the tonga unloaded and our effects placed in the verandah, the bullocks untackled and turned out among the long rank grass. At length an old man in dirty ragged clothes, and with a villainous expression of countenance, appeared from some back cook-house, and seemed anything but pleased to see us. When Abdul told him of our intention of occupying the house, he would not hear of it. "The bungalow was out of repair; it had not been opened for years; it was full of rats; it was unhealthy; plenty fever coming. We must go on to Chanda."

Naturally we declined his hospitable suggestion.

"Was he the khansamah—caretaker of the place?" we inquired imperiously.

"Yees," he admitted with a grunt.

"Drawing government pay, and refusing to open a government travellers' bungalow!" screamed Julia. "Let us have no more of this nonsense; open the house at once and get it ready for us, or I shall report you to the commissioner sahib."

The khansamah gave her an evil look, said "Missus please," shrugged his shoulders and hobbled away—as we hoped, to get the key; but after waiting ten minutes we sent Abdul to search for him, and found that he had departed—his lair was empty. There was nothing for it but to break the padlock on the door, which Abdul effected with a stone, and as soon as the door moved slowly back on its hinges Julia and I hurried in. What a dark, damp place! What a smell of earth, and what numbers of bats; they flew right in our faces as we stood in the doorway and tried to make out the interior. Abdul and the bullock-man quickly removed the shutters and let in the light, and then we beheld the usual dâk sitting-room—a table, chairs, and two charpoys (native beds), and an old pair of candlesticks; the table and chairs were covered with mould; cobwebs hung from the ceiling in dreadful festoons, and the walls were streaked with dreary green stains. I could not restrain an involuntary shudder as I looked about me rather blankly.

"I should think this *was* an unhealthy place!" I remarked to Julia. "It looks feverish; and see—the jungle comes right up to the back verandah; fever plants, castor-oil plants, young bamboos, all growing up to the very walls."

"It will do very well for to-night," she returned. "Come out and walk down the road whilst Abdul and the bullock-man clean out the rooms and get dinner. Abdul is a wonderful man—and we won't know the place in an hour's time; it's just the same as any other travellers' bungalow, only it has been neglected for years. I shall certainly report that old wretch! The *idea* of a dâk bungalow caretaker re-

fusing admittance and running away with the key! What is
the name of this place?" she asked, deliberately taking out
her pocket-book; "did you hear?"

"Yes; I believe it is called Dakor."

"Ah, well! I shall not forget to tell Frank about the way
we were treated at Dakor bungalow."

The red, red sun had set at last—gone down, as it were,
abruptly behind the flat horizon; the air began to feel chilly,
and the owl and the jackal were commencing to make
themselves heard, so we sauntered back to the bungalow,
and found it indeed transformed: swept and garnished,
and clean. The table was neatly laid for dinner, and one of
our own fine hurricane lamps blazed upon it; our beds had
been made up with our rugs and blankets, one at either
end of the room; hot water and towels were prepared in a
bath-room, and we saw a roaring fire in the cook-house in
the jungle. Dinner, consisting of a sudden-death fowl, curry,
bread, and *pâté de foie gras*, was, to our unjaded palates,
an excellent meal. Our spirits rose to normal, the result of
food and light, and we declared to one another that this
old bungalow was a capital find, and that it was really both
comfortable and cheerful, despite a slight *arrière-pensée* of
earth in the atmosphere!

Before going to bed we explored the next room, a smaller
one than that we occupied, and empty save for a rickety
camp table, which held some dilapidated crockery and a
press. Need you ask if we opened this press? The press smelt
strongly of mushrooms, and contained a man's topee, inch-
deep with mould, a tiffin basket, and the bungalow visitors'
book. We carried this away with us to read at leisure, for the
visitors' book in dâk bungalows occasionally contains some
rather amusing observations. There was nothing funny in
this musty old volume! Merely a statement of who came,
and how long they stayed, and what they paid, with a few

remarks, not by any means complimentary to the khansa-mah: "A dirty, lazy rascal," said one; "A murderous-looking ruffian," said another; "An insolent, drunken hound," said a third—the last entry was dated seven years previously.

"Let us write our names," said Julia, taking out her pencil; " 'Mrs. Goodchild and Mrs. Loyd, December 23rd. Bungalow deserted, and very dirty khansamah.' What shall we say?" she asked, glancing at me interrogatively.

"Why, there he is!" I returned with a little jump; and there he was sure enough, gazing in through the window. It was the face of some malicious animal, more than the face of a man that glowered out beneath his filthy red turban. His eyes glared and rolled as if they would leave their sockets; his teeth were fangs, like dogs' teeth, and stood out almost perpendicularly from his hideous mouth. He surveyed us for a few seconds in savage silence, and then melted away into the surrounding darkness as suddenly as he appeared.

"He reminds me of the Cheshire cat in *Alice in Wonder-land*," said Julia with would-be facetiousness, but I noticed that she looked rather pale.

"Let us have the shutters up at once," I replied, "and have them well barred and the doors bolted. That man looked as if he could cut our throats."

In a very short time the house was made fast. Abdul and the bullock-man spread their mats in the front verandah, and Julia and I retired for the night. Before going to bed we had a controversy about the lamp. I wished to keep it burning all night (I am a coward at heart), but Julia would not hear of this—impossible for her to sleep with a light in the room—and in the end I was compelled to be content with a candle and matches on a chair beside me. I fell asleep very soon. I fancy I must have slept long and soundly, when I was awoke by a bright light shining in my eyes. So, after the ridiculous fuss she had made, Julia *had* lit the candle after all! This was my first thought, but when I was fully awake I found I was mistaken, or dreaming. No, I was not dreaming, for I pinched my arm and rubbed my eyes. There was a man in the room, apparently another traveller, who appeared to be totally unaware of our vicinity, and to have made himself completely at home. A gun-case, a tiffin basket, a bundle of pillows and rugs—the usual Indian traveller's belongings—lay carelessly scattered about on the chairs and the floor. I leant up on my elbow and gazed at the intruder in amazement. He did not notice me, no more than if I had no existence; true, my charpoy was in a corner of the room and rather in the shade, so was Julia's. Julia was sound asleep and (low be it spoken) snoring. The stranger was writing a letter at the table facing me. Both candles were drawn up close to him, and threw a searching light upon his features. He was young and good-looking, but very, very pale; possibly he had just recovered from some long illness. I could not see his eyes, they were bent upon the paper before him; his hands, I noticed, were well shaped, white, and very thin. He wore a signet-ring on the third finger of the left hand, and was dressed with a care and finish not often met with in the jungle. He wore some kind of light Norfolk jacket and a blue bird's-eye tie. In front of him stood an open despatch-box, very shabby and scratched, and I could see that the upper tray contained a stout roundabout bag, presumably full of rupees, a thick roll of notes, and a gold watch. When I had deliberately taken in every item, the unutterable calmness of this stranger, thus establishing himself in our room, came home to me most forcibly, and clearing my throat I coughed—a clear decided cough of expostulation, to draw his attention to the enormity of the situation. It had no effect—he must be stone-deaf! He went on writing as indefatigably as ever. What he was writing was evidently a pleasant theme, possibly a love-letter, for he smiled as he scribbled. All at once I observed that the door was ajar. Two faces were peering in—a strange servant in a yellow turban, with cruel, greedy eyes, and *the khansamah*! Their gaze was riveted on the open despatch-box, the money, the roll of notes, and the watch. Presently the traveller's servant stole up behind his master noiselessly, and seemed to hold his breath; he drew a long knife from his sleeve. At this moment the stranger raised his eyes and looked at me. Oh, what a sad, strange look! a look of appeal. The next instant I saw the flash of the knife—it was buried in his back; he fell forward over his letter with a crash and a groan, and all was darkness. I tried to scream, but I could not. My tongue seemed paralysed. I covered my head up in the clothes, and oh, how my heart beat! thump, thump, thump—surely they must hear it, and discover me. Half suffocated, at length I ventured to peer out for a second. All was still, black darkness. There was nothing to be seen, but much to be heard—the dragging of a heavy body, a *dead* body, across the room; then, after an appreciable pause, the sounds of digging out-side the bungalow. Finally, the splashing of water—*some one washing the floor*. When I awoke the next morning, or came to myself—for I believe I had fainted—daylight was demanding admittance at every crevice in the shutters; night, its dark hours and its horrors, was past. The torture, the agony of fear, that had held me captive, had now released me, and, worn out, I fell fast asleep. It was actually nine o'clock when I opened my eyes. Julia was standing over me and shaking me vigorously, and saying, "Nellie, Nellie, wake; I've been up and out this two hours; I've seen the head man of the village."

"Have you?" I assented sleepily.

"Yes, and he says there are no bullocks to be had until to-morrow; we must pass another night here."

"Never!" I almost shrieked. "Never! Oh, Julia, I've had such a night. I've seen a murder!" And straightway I commenced, and told her of my awful experiences. "That khansamah murdered him. He is buried just outside the front step," I concluded tearfully. "Sooner than stay here another night I'll *walk* to Chanda."

"Ghosts! murders! walk to Chanda!" she echoed scornfully. "Why, you silly girl, did I not sleep here in this very room, and sleep as sound as a top? It was all the *pâté de foie gras*. You *know* it never agrees with you."

"I know nothing about *pâté de foie gras*," I answered angrily; "but I know what I saw. Sooner than sleep another night in this room I'd *die*. I might as well—for such another night would kill me!"

Bath, breakfast, and Julia brought me round to a certain extent. I thought better of tearing off to Chanda alone and on foot, especially as we heard (per coolie) that our respective husbands would be with us the next morning—Christmas Day. We spent the day cooking, exploring the country, and writing for the English mail. As night fell, I became more and more nervous, and less amenable to Julia and Julia's jokes. I would sleep in the verandah; either there, or in the compound. In the bungalow again—never. An old witch of a native woman, who was helping Abdul to cook, agreed to place her mat in the same locality as my mattress, and Julia Goodchild valiantly occupied the big room within, alone. In the middle of the night I and my protector were awoke by the most piercing, frightful shrieks. We lit a candle and ran into the bungalow, and found Julia lying on the floor in a dead faint. She did not come round for more than an hour, and when she opened her eyes she gazed about her with a shudder and displayed symptoms of going off again, so I instantly hunted up our flask and administered some raw brandy, and presently she found her tongue and attacked the old native woman quite viciously.

"Tell the truth about this place!" she said fiercely. "What is it that is here, in this room?"

"Devils," was the prompt and laconic reply.

"Nonsense! Murder has been done here; tell the truth."

"How I knowing?" she whined. "I only poor native woman."

"An English sahib was murdered here seven years ago; stabbed and dragged out, and buried under the steps."

"Ah, bah! ah, bah! How I telling? this not my country," she wailed most piteously.

"Tell all you know," persisted Julia. "You *do* know! My husband is coming to-day; he is a police officer. You had better tell me than him."

After much whimpering and hand-wringing, we extracted the following information in jerks and quavers:—

The bungalow had a bad name, no one ever entered it, and in spite of the wooden shutters there were lights in the windows every night up to twelve o'clock. One day (so the villagers said), many years ago, a young sahib came to this bungalow and stayed three days. He was alone. He was in the Forest Department. The last evening he sent his horses and servants on to Chanda, and said he would follow in the morning after having some shooting, he and his "boy"; but though his people waited two weeks, he never appeared—was never seen again. The khansamah declared that he and his servant had left in the early morning, but no one met them. The khansamah became suddenly very rich; said he had found a treasure; also, be sold a fine gold watch in Jubbulpore, and took to drink. He had a bad name, and the bungalow had a bad name. No one would stay there more than one night, and no one had stayed there for many years till we came. The khansamah lived in the cook-house; he was always drunk. People said there were devils in the house, and no one would go near it after sundown. This was all she knew.

"Poor fellow, he was so good-looking!" sighed Julia when we were alone. "Poor fellow, and he was murdered and buried here!"

"So I told you," I replied, "and you would not believe me, but insisted on staying to see for yourself."

"I wish I had not—oh, I wish I had not! I shall never, never forget last night as long as I live."

"That must have been *his* topee and tiffin basket that we saw in the press," I exclaimed. "As soon as your husband comes, we will tell him everything, and set him on the track of the murderers."

Breakfast on Christmas morning was a very doleful meal; our nerves were completely shattered by our recent experiences, and we could only rouse ourselves up to offer a very melancholy sort of welcome to our two husbands, when they cantered briskly into the compound. In reply to their eager questions as to the cause of our lugubrious appearance, pale faces, and general air of mourning, we favoured them with a vivid description of our two nights in the bungalow. Of course, they were loudly, rudely in-credulous, and, of course, *we* were very angry; vainly we re-stated our case, and displayed the old topee and tiffin basket; they merely laughed still more heartily and talked of "nightmare", and gave themselves such airs of offensive superiority, that Julia's soul flew to arms.

"Look here," she cried passionately, "*I* laughed at Nellie as you laugh at us. We will go out of this compound, whilst you two dig, or get people to dig, below the front verandah and in front of the steps, and if you don't find the skeleton of a murdered man, then you may laugh at us for ever."

With Julia impulse meant action, and before I could say three words I was out of the compound, with my arm wedged under hers; we went and sat on a little stone bridge within a stone's throw of the bungalow, glum and silent enough. What a Christmas Day! Half an hour's delay was as much as Julia's patience could brook. We then retraced our steps and discovered what seemed to be the whole village in the dâk bungalow compound. Frank came hurrying towards us, waving us frantically away. No need for questions; his face was enough. They had found it.

❋

Frank Goodchild had known him—he was in his own department, a promising and most popular young fellow; his name was Gordon Forbes; he had been missed but never traced, and there was a report that he had been gored and killed in the jungle by a wild buffalo. In the same grave was found the battered despatch-box, by which the skeleton was identified. Mr. Goodchild and my husband re-interred the body under a tree, and read the Burial Service over it, Nellie and I and all the village patriarchs attending as mourners. The khansamah was eagerly searched for—alas! in vain. He disappeared from that part of the country, and was said to have been devoured by a tiger in the Jhanas jungles; but this is too good to be true. We left the hateful bungalow with all speed that same afternoon, and spent the remainder of the Christmas Day at Chanda; it was the least merry Christmas we ever remembered. The Goodchilds and ourselves have subscribed and placed a granite cross, with his name and the date of his death, over Gordon Forbes's lonely grave, and the news of the discovery of the skeleton was duly forwarded to the proper authorities, and also to the unfortunate young man's relations, and to these were sent the despatch-box, letters, and ring.

Mrs. Duff was full of curiosity concerning our trip. We informed her that we spent Christmas at Chanda, as we had originally intended, with our husbands, that they had provided an excellent dinner of black buck and jungle fowl, that the plum-pudding surpassed all expectations: but we never told her a word about our two nights' halt at Dakor bungalow.

TO LET

"List, list, O list!" – Hamlet, Act I.

Some years ago, when I was a slim young spin, I came out to India to live with my brother Tom: he and I were members of a large and somewhat impecunious family, and I do not think my mother was sorry to have one of her four grown-up daughters thus taken off her hands. Tom's wife, Aggie, had been at school with my eldest sister; we had known and liked her all our lives, and regarded her as one of ourselves; and as she and the children were at home when Tom's letter was received, and his offer accepted, she helped me to choose my slender outfit, with judgment, zeal, and taste; endowed me with several pretty additions to my wardrobe; superintended the fitting of my gowns and the trying on of my hats, with most sympathetic interest, and finally escorted me out to Lucknow, under her own wing, and installed me in the only spare room in her comfortable bungalow in Dilkousha.

My sister-in-law is a pretty little brunette, rather pale, with dark hair, brilliant black eyes, a resolute mouth, and a bright, intelligent expression. She is orderly, trim, feverishly energetic, and seems to live every moment of her life. Her children, her wardrobe, her house, her servants, and last, not least, her husband, are all models in their way; and yet she has plenty of time for tennis, and dancing, and talking and walking. She is, undoubtedly, a remarkably talented little creature, and especially prides herself on her nerve, and her power of will, or will power. I suppose they are the same thing? and I am sure they are all the same to Tom, who worships the sole of her small slipper. Strictly between ourselves, she is the ruling member of the family, and turns her lord and master round her little finger. Tom is big and fair (of course), the opposite to his wife, quiet, rather easy-going and inclined to be indolent; but Aggie rouses him up, and pushes him to the front, and keeps him there. She knows all about his department, his prospects of promotion, his prospects of furlough, of getting acting appointments, and so on, even better than he does himself. The chief of Tom's department—have I said that Tom is in the Irritation Office?—has placed it solemnly on record that he considers little Mrs. Shandon a surprisingly clever woman. The two children, Bob and Tor, are merry, oppressively active monkeys, aged three and five years respectively. As for myself, I am tall, fair—and I wish I could add pretty! but this is a true story. My eyes are blue, my teeth are white, my hair is red—alas, a blazing red; and I was, at this period, nineteen years of age; and now I think I have given a sufficient outline of the whole family.

We arrived at Lucknow in November, when the cold weather is delightful, and everything was delightful to me. The bustle and life of a great Indian station, the novelty of my surroundings, the early morning rides, picnics down the river, and dances at the "Chutter Munzil", made me look upon Lucknow as a paradise on earth; and in this light I still regarded it, until a great change came over the temperature, and the month of April introduced me to red-hot winds, sleepless nights, and the intolerable "brain fever" bird. Aggie had made up her mind definitely on one subject: we were not to go away to the hills until the rains. Tom could only get two months' leave (July and August), and she did not intend to leave him to grill on the plains alone. As for herself and the children—not to speak of me—we had all come out from home so recently that we did not require a change. The trip to Europe had made a vast hole in the family stocking, and she wished to economise; and who can economise with two establishments in full swing? Tell me this, ye Anglo-Indian matrons? With a large, cool bungalow, plenty of punkhas, khuskhus tatties, ice, and a thermantidote, surely we could manage to brave May and June—at any rate the attempt was made. Gradually the hills drained Lucknow week by week; family after family packed up, warned us of our folly in remaining on the plains, offered to look for houses for us, and left by the night mail. By the middle of May, the place was figuratively empty. Nothing can be more dreary than a large station in the hot weather—unless it is an equally forsaken hill station in the depths of winter, when the mountains are covered with snow, the mall no longer resounds with gay voices and the tramp of Jampanies, but is visited by bears and panthers, and the houses are closed, and, as it were, put to bed in straw! As for Lucknow in the summer, it was a melancholy spot; the public gardens were deserted, the chairs at the Chutter Munzil stood empty, the very bands had gone to the hills! the shops were shut, the baked white roads, no longer thronged with carriages and bamboo carts, gave ample room to the humble ekka, or a Dhobie's meagre donkey, shuffling along in the dust.

Of course we were not the *only* people remaining in the place, grumbling at the heat and dust and life in general; but there can be no sociability with the thermometer above 100° in the shade. Through the long, long Indian day we sat and gasped, in darkened rooms, and consumed quantities of "Nimbo pegs", i.e. limes and soda water, and listened to the fierce hot wind roaring along the road and driving the roasted leaves before it; and in the evening, when the sun had set, we went for a melancholy drive through the Wingfield Park, or round by Martiniere College, and met our friends at the library, and compared sensations and thermometers. The season was exceptionally bad (but people say that every year), and presently Bobby and Tor began to fade: their little white faces and listless eyes appealed to Aggie as Tom's anxious expostulations had never done. "Yes, they must go to the hills with *me*." But this idea I repudiated at once; I refused to undertake the responsibility—I, who could scarcely speak a word to the servants—who had no experience! Then Bobbie had a bad go of fever—intermittent fever; the beginning of the end to his alarmed mother; the end being represented by a large gravestone! She now became as firmly determined to go, as she had previously been resolved to stay; but it was so late in the season to take a house. Alas, alas, for the beautiful tempting advertisements in the *Pioneer*, which we had seen and scorned! Aggie wrote to a friend in a certain hill station, called (for this occasion only) "Kantia", and Tom wired to a house agent, who triumphantly replied by letter, that there was not *one* unlet bungalow on his books. This missive threw us into the depths of despair; there seemed no alternative but a hill hotel, and the usual quarters that await the last comers, and the proverbial welcome for children and dogs (we had only four); but the next day brought us good news from Aggie's friend Mrs. Chalmers.

Dear Mrs. Shandon (she said),

I received your letter, and went at once to Cursitjee, the agent. Every hole and corner up here seems full, and he had not a single house to let. To-day I had a note from him, saying that Briarwood is vacant; the people who took it are not coming up, they have gone to Naini Tal. You *are* in luck. I have just been out to see the house, and have secured it for you. It is a mile and a half from the club, but I know that you and your sister are capital walkers. I envy you. Such a charming place—two sitting-rooms, four bedrooms, four bath-rooms, a hall, servants' go-downs, stabling, and a splendid view from a very pretty garden, and only Rs. 800 for the season! Why, I am paying Rs. 1000 for a very inferior house, with scarcely a stick of furniture and no view. I feel so proud of myself, and I am longing to show you my treasure-trove. Telegraph when you start, and I shall have a milkman in waiting and fires in all the rooms.

Yours sincerely,
Edith Chalmers.

We now looked upon Mrs. Chalmers as our best and dearest friend, and began to get under way at once. A long journey in India is a serious business, when the party comprises two ladies, two children, two ayahs, and five other servants, three fox terriers, a mongoose, and a Persian cat—all these animals going to the hills for the benefit of their health—not to speak of a ton of luggage, including crockery and lamps, a cottage piano, a goat, and a pony. Aggie and I, the children, one ayah, two terriers, the cat and mongoose, our bedding and pillows, the tiffin basket and ice basket, were all stowed into one compartment, and I must confess that the journey was truly miserable. The heat was stifling, despite the water tatties. One of the terriers had a violent dispute with the cat, and the cat had a difference with the mongoose, and Bob and Tor had a pitched battle; more than once I actually wished myself back in Lucknow. I was most truly thankful to wake one morning, to find myself under the shadow of the Himalayas—not a mighty, snow-clad range of everlasting hills, but merely the spurs—the moderate slopes, covered with scrub, loose shale, and jungle, and deceitful little trickling watercourses. We sent the servants on ahead, whilst we rested at the dâk bungalow near the railway station, and then followed them at our leisure. We accomplished the ascent in dandies—open kind of boxes, half box, half chair, carried on the shoulders of four men. This was an entirely novel sensation to me, and at first an agreeable one, so long as the slopes were moderate, and the paths wide; but the higher we went, the narrower became the path, the steeper the naked precipice; and as my coolies would walk at the extreme edge, with the utmost indifference to my frantic appeals to "Bector! Bector!"—and would change poles at the most agonising corners—my feelings were very mixed, especially when droves of loose pack ponies came thundering downhill, with no respect for the rights of the road. Late at night we passed through Kantia, and arrived at Briarwood, far too weary to be critical. Fires were blazing, supper was prepared, and we despatched it in haste, and most thankfully went to bed and slept soundly, as any one would do who had spent thirty-six hours in a crowded compartment, and ten in a cramped wooden case.

The next morning, rested and invigorated, we set out on a tour of inspection; and it is almost worth while to undergo a certain amount of baking in the sweltering heat of the lower regions, in order to enjoy those deep first draughts of cool hill air, instead of a stifling, dust-laden atmosphere; and to appreciate the green valleys and blue hills, by force of contrast to the far-stretching, eye-smarting, white glaring roads, that intersect the burnt-up plains—roads and plains, that even the pariah abandons, salamander though he be!

To our delight and surprise, Mrs. Chalmers had by no means overdrawn the advantages of our new abode. The bungalow was solidly built of stone, two storied, and ample in size. It stood on a kind of shelf, cut out of the hillside, and was surrounded by a pretty flower garden, full of roses, fuchsias, and carnations. The high road passed the gate, from which the avenue descended, direct to the entrance door, at the end of the house, and from whence ran a long passage.

Off this passage three rooms opened to the right, all looking south, and all looking into a deep, delightful, flagged, verandah. The stairs were very steep. At the head of them, the passage and rooms were repeated. There were small nooks, and dressing-rooms, and convenient out-houses, and plenty of good water; but the glory of Briarwood was undoubtedly its verandah: it was fully twelve feet wide, roofed with zinc, and overhung a precipice of a thousand feet—not a startlingly sheer khud, but a tolerably straight descent of grey-blue shale, rocks, and low jungle. From it there was a glorious view, across a valley, far away, to the snowy range. It opened at one end into the avenue, and was not inclosed; but at the side next the precipice, there was a stout wooden railing, with netting at the bottom, for the safety of too enterprising dogs or children. A charming spot, despite its rather bold situation; and as Aggie and I sat in it, surveying the scenery and inhaling the pure hill air, and watching Bob and Tor tearing up and down, playing horses, we said to one another that "the verandah alone was worth half the rent".

"It's absurdly cheap," exclaimed my sister-in-law complacently. "I wish you saw the hovel *I* had, at Simla, for the same rent. I wonder if it is feverish, or badly drained, or what?"

"Perhaps it has a ghost," I suggested facetiously; and at such an absurd idea we both went into peals of laughter.

At this moment Mrs. Chalmers appeared, brisk, rosy, and breathlessly benevolent, having walked over from Kantia.

"So you have found it," she said as we shook hands. "I said nothing about this delicious verandah! I thought I would keep it as a surprise. I did not say a word too much for Briarwood, did I?"

"Not half enough," we returned rapturously; and presently we went in a body, armed with a list from the agent, and proceeded to go over the house and take stock of its contents.

"It's not a bit like a *hill* furnished house," boasted Mrs. Chalmers, with a glow of pride, as she looked round the drawing-room; "carpets, curtains, solid, *very* solid chairs, and Berlin wool-worked screens, a card-table, and any quantity of pictures."

"Yes, don't they look like family portraits?" I suggested, as we gazed at them. There was one of an officer in faded water colours, another of his wife, two of a previous generation in oils and amply gilded frames, two sketches of an English country house, and some framed photographs—groups of grinning cricketers, or wedding guests. All the rooms were well, almost handsomely, furnished in an old-fashioned style. There was no scarcity of wardrobes, looking-glasses, or even armchairs, in the bedrooms, and the pantry was fitted out—a most singular circumstance—with a large supply of handsome glass and china, lamps, old moderators, coffee and teapots, plated side dishes, and candlesticks, cooking utensils and spoons and forks, wine coasters and a cake-basket. These articles were all let with the house (much to our amazement), provided we were responsible for the same. The china was spode, the plate old family heirlooms, with a crest—a winged horse—on everything, down to the very mustard spoons.

"The people who own this house must be lunatics," remarked Aggie, as she peered round the pantry; "fancy hiring out one's best family plate, and good old china! And I saw some ancient music-books in the drawing-room, and there is a side saddle in the bottle khana."

"My dear, the people who owned this house are dead," explained Mrs. Chalmers. "I heard all about them last evening from Mrs. Starkey."

"Oh, is *she* up there?" exclaimed Aggie, somewhat fretfully.

"Yes, her husband is cantonment magistrate. This house belonged to an old retired colonel and his wife. They and his niece lived here. These were all their belongings. They died within a short time of one another, and the old man left a queer will, to say that the house was to remain precisely as they left it for twenty years, and at the end of that time, it was to be sold and all the property dispersed. Mrs. Starkey says she is sure that he never intended it to be *let,* but the heir-at-law insists on that, and is furious at the terms of the will."

"Well, it is a very good thing for us," remarked Aggie; "we are as comfortable here, as if we were in our own house: there is a stove in the kitchen, there are nice boxes for firewood in every room, clocks, real hair mattresses—in short, it is as you said, a treasure trove."

We set to work to modernise the drawing-room with phoolkaries, Madras muslin curtains, photograph screens and frames, and such-like portable articles. We placed the piano across a corner, arranged flowers in some handsome Dresden china vases, and entirely altered and improved the character of the room. When Aggie had despatched a most glowing description of our new quarters to Tom, and when we had had tiffin, we set off to walk into Kantia to put our names down at the library, and to inquire for letters at the post- office. Aggie met a good many acquaintances—who does not, who has lived five years in India in the same district?

Among them Mrs. Starkey, an elderly lady with a prominent nose and goggle eyes, who greeted her loudly across the reading-room table, in this agreeable fashion:

"And so you have come up after *all*, Mrs. Shandon. Some one told me that you meant to remain below, but I knew you never could be so wicked as to keep your poor little children in that heat." Then coming round and dropping into a chair beside her, she said, "And I suppose this young lady is your sister-in-law?"

Mrs. Starkey eyed me critically, evidently appraising my chances in the great marriage market. She herself had settled her own two daughters most satisfactorily, and had now nothing to do, but interest herself in other people's affairs.

"Yes," acquiesced Aggie; "Miss Shandon—Mrs. Starkey."

"And so you have taken Briarwood?"

"Yes, we have been most lucky to get it."

"I hope you will think so, at the end of three months," observed Mrs. Starkey, with a significant pursing of her lips. "Mrs. Chalmers is a stranger up here, or she would not have been in such a hurry to jump at it."

"Why, what is the matter with it?" inquired Aggie. "It is well built, well furnished, well situated, and very cheap."

"That's just it—*suspiciously* cheap. Why, my dear Mrs. Shandon, if there was not something against it, it would let for two hundred rupees a month. Common sense would tell you that!"

"And what is against it?"

"It's haunted! There you have the reason in two words."

"Is that all? I was afraid it was the drains. I don't believe in ghosts and haunted houses. What are we supposed to see?"

"Nothing," retorted Mrs. Starkey, who seemed a good deal nettled at our smiling incredulity.

"Nothing!" with an exasperating laugh.

"No, but you will make up for it in hearing. Not now—you are all right for the next six weeks—but after the monsoon breaks, I give you a week at Briarwood. No one would stand it longer, and indeed you might as well bespeak your rooms at Cooper's Hotel *now*. There is always a rush up here in July, by the two months' leave people, and you will be poked into some wretched go-down."

Aggie laughed, rather a careless ironical little laugh, and said, "Thank you, Mrs. Starkey; but I think we will stay on where we are—at any rate for the present."

"Of course it will be as *you* please. What do you think of the verandah?" she inquired, with a curious smile.

"I think, as I was saying to Susan, that it is worth half the rent of the house."

"And in my opinion the house is worth double rent without it;" and with this enigmatic remark, she rose, and sailed away.

"Horrid old frump!" exclaimed Aggie, as we walked home in the starlight. "She is jealous and angry that she did not get Briarwood *herself*—I know her so well. She is always hinting, and repeating stories about the nicest people—always decrying your prettiest dress, or your best servant."

We soon forgot all about Mrs. Starkey, and her dismal prophecy, being too gay, and too busy, to give her, or it, a thought. We had so many engagements—tennis-parties and tournaments, picnics, concerts, dances, and little dinners. We ourselves gave occasional afternoon teas in the verandah—using the best spode cups and saucers, and the old silver cake-basket—and were warmly complimented on our good fortune in securing such a charming house and garden. One day the children discovered, to their great joy, that the old chowkidar belonging to the bungalow possessed an African grey parrot—a rare bird indeed in India; he had a battered Europe cage, doubtless a remnant of better days, and swung on his ring, looking up at us inquiringly, out of his impudent little black eyes.

The parrot had been the property of the former inmates of Briarwood, and as it was a long-lived creature, had survived its master and mistress, and was boarded out with the chowkidar, at one rupee per month.

The chowkidar willingly carried the cage into the verandah, where the bird seemed perfectly at home.

We got a little table for its cage, and the children were delighted with him, as he swung to and fro, with a bit of cake in his wrinkled claw.

Presently he startled us all by suddenly calling "Lucy", in a voice that was as distinct as if it had come from a human throat. "Pretty Lucy—Lu–cy."

"That must have been the niece," said Aggie. "I expect she was the original of that picture over the chimney-piece in your room; she looks like a Lucy."

It was a large, framed, half-length photograph of a very pretty girl, in a white dress, with gigantic open sleeves. The ancient parrot talked incessantly now that he had been restored to society; he whistled for the dogs, and brought them flying to his summons—to his great satisfaction, and their equally great indignation. He called "Qui hye" so naturally, in a lady's shrill soprano, or a gruff male bellow, that I have no doubt our servants would have liked to have wrung his neck. He coughed and expectorated like an old gentleman, and whined like a puppy, and mewed like a cat, and, I am sorry to add, sometimes swore like a trooper; but his most constant cry was, "Lucy, where are you, pretty Lucy—Lucy—Lu–cy?"

Aggie and I went to various picnics, but to that given by the Chalmers (in honour of Mr. Chalmers' brother Charlie, a captain in a Ghoorka regiment, just come up to Kantia on leave) Aggie was un-avoidably absent. Tor had a little touch of fever, and she did not like to leave him; but I went under my hostess's care, and expected to enjoy myself immensely. Alas! on that selfsame afternoon, the long-expected monsoon broke, and we were nearly drowned! We rode to the selected spot, five miles from Kantia, laughing and chattering, indifferent to the big blue-black clouds that came slowly, but surely, sailing up from below; it was a way they had had for days, and nothing had come of it! We spread the table-cloth, boiled the kettle, unpacked the hampers, in spite of sharp gusts of wind and warning rumbling thunder. Just as we had commenced to reap the reward of our exertions, there fell a few huge drops, followed by a vivid flash, and then a tremendous crash of thunder, like a whole park of artillery, that seemed to shake the mountains—and after this the deluge. In less than a minute we were soaked through; we hastily gathered up the table-cloth by its four ends, gave it to the coolies, and fled. It was all I could do to stand against the wind; only for Captain Chalmers I believe I would have been blown away; as it was, I lost my hat, it was whirled into space. Mrs. Chalmers lost her boa, and Mrs. Starkey, not merely her bonnet, but some portion of her hair. We were truly in a wretched plight, the water streaming down our faces, and squelching in our boots; the little trickling mountain rivulets were now like racing seas of turbid water; the lightning was almost blinding; the trees rocked dangerously, and lashed one another with their quivering branches. I had never been out in such a storm before, and sincerely hope I never may again. We reached Kantia more dead than alive, and Mrs. Chalmers sent an express to Aggie, and kept me till the next day. After raining as it only can rain in the Himalayas, the weather cleared, the sun shone, and I rode home in borrowed plumes, full of my adventures, and in the highest spirits. I found Aggie sitting over the fire in the drawing-room, looking ghastly white: that was nothing uncommon; but terribly depressed, which was most unusual.

"I am afraid you have neuralgia?" I said, as I kissed her.

She nodded, and made no reply. "How is Tor?" I inquired, as I drew a chair up to the fire.

"Better—quite well."

"Any news—any letter?"

"Not a word—not a line."

"Has anything happened to Pip"—Pip was a fox-terrier, renowned for having the shortest tail and being the most impertinent dog in Lucknow—"or the mongoose?"

"No, you silly girl! Why do you ask such ridiculous questions?"

"I was afraid something was amiss; you seem rather down on your luck."

Aggie shrugged her shoulders, and then said, "Pray, what put such an absurd idea into your head? Tell me all about the picnic," and she began to talk rapidly, and to ask me various questions; but I observed that once she had set me going— no difficult task—her attention flagged, her eyes wandered from my face to the fire. She was not listening to half I said, and my most thrilling descriptions were utterly lost on this indifferent, abstracted little creature! I noticed from this time, that she had become strangely nervous (for her). She invited herself to the share of half my bed; she was restless, *distrait*, and even irritable; and when I was asked out to spend the day, dispensed with my company with an alacrity that was by no means flattering. Formerly, of an evening she used to herd the children home at sundown, and tear me away from the delights of the reading-room at seven o'clock; now she hung about the library, until almost the last moment, until it was time to put out the lamps, and kept the children with her, making transparent pretexts for their company. Often we did not arrive at home till half-past eight o'clock. I made no objections to these late hours, neither did Charlie Chalmers, who often walked back with us and remained to dinner. I was amazed to notice that Aggie seemed delighted to have his company, for she had always expressed a rooted aversion to what she called "tame young men", and here was this new acquaintance dining with us, at least twice a week!

About a month after the picnic we had a spell of dreadful weather—thunderstorms accompanied by torrents. One pouring afternoon, Aggie and I were cowering over the drawing-room fire, whilst the rain came fizzing down among the logs, and ran in rivers off the roof, and out of the spouts. There had been no going out that day, and we were feeling rather flat and dull, as we sat in a kind of ghostly twilight, with all outdoor objects swallowed up in mist, listening to the violent battering of the rain on the zinc verandah, and the storm which was growling round the hills.

"Oh, for a visitor!" I exclaimed; "but no one but a fish, or a lunatic, would be out on such an evening."

"No one, indeed," echoed Aggie, in a melancholy tone. "We may as well draw the curtains, and have in the lamp and tea to cheer us up."

She had scarcely finished speaking, when I heard the brisk trot of a horse along the road.

It stopped at the gate, and came rapidly down our avenue. I heard the wet gravel crunching under his hoofs, and—yes, a man's cheery whistle. My heart jumped, and I half rose from my chair. It must be Charlie Chalmers braving the elements to see me!—such, I must confess, was my incredible vanity! He did not stop at the front door as usual, but rode straight into the verandah, which afforded ample room, and shelter for half a dozen mounted men.

"Aggie," I said eagerly, "do you hear? It must be—"

I paused, my tongue silenced, by the awful pallor of her face, and the expression of her eyes, as she sat with her little hands clutching the arms of her chair, and her whole figure bent forward in an attitude of listening—an attitude of rigid terror.

"What is it, Aggie?" I said. "Are you ill?"

As I spoke, the horse's hoofs made a loud clattering noise on the stone-paved verandah outside, and a man's voice—a young man's eager voice—called, "Lucy."

Instantly a chair near the writing-table was pushed back, and some one went quickly to the window—a French one—and bungled for a moment with the fastening. I always had a difficulty with that window *myself*. Aggie and I were within the bright circle of the firelight, but the rest of the room was dim, and outside the streaming grey sky was spasmodically illuminated by occasional vivid flashes, that lit up the surrounding hills as if it were daylight. The trampling of impatient hoofs, and the rattling of a door-handle, were the only sounds that were audible for a few breathless seconds; but during those seconds Pip, bristling like a porcupine, and trembling violently in every joint, had sprung off my lap and crawled abjectly under Aggie's chair, seemingly in a transport of fear. The door was opened audibly, and a cold, icy blast swept in, that seemed to freeze my very heart, and made me shiver from head to foot. At this moment there came, with a sinister blue glare, the most vivid flash of lightning I ever saw. It lit up the whole room, which was empty save for ourselves, and was instantly followed by a clap of thunder, that caused my knees to knock together, and that terrified me and filled me with horror. It evidently terrified the horse too; there was a violent plunge, a clattering of hoofs on the stones, a sudden loud crash of smashing timber, a woman's long, loud, piercing shriek, which stopped the very beating of my heart, and then a frenzied struggle in the cruel, crumbling, treacherous shale, the rattle of loose stones, and the hollow roar of something sliding down the precipice.

I rushed to the door and tore it open, with that awful despairing cry still ringing in my ears. The verandah was empty; there was not a soul to be seen, or a sound to be heard, save the rain on the roof.

"Aggie," I screamed, "come here! Some one has gone over the verandah, and down the khud! You heard him."

"Yes," she said, following me out; "but come in—come in."

"I believe it was Charlie Chalmers"—shaking her violently as I spoke. "He has been killed—killed—killed! And you stand, and do nothing. Send people! Let us go ourselves! Bearer! Ayah! Khitmatgar!" I cried, raising my voice.

"Hush! It was *not* Charlie Chalmers," she said, vainly endeavouring to draw me into the drawing-room. "Come in—come in."

"No, no!" pushing her away, and wringing my hands. "How cruel you are! How inhuman! There is a path. Let us go at once—at once!"

"You need not trouble yourself, Susan," she interrupted; "and you need not cry and tremble;—*they* will bring him up. What you heard was supernatural; it was not real."

"No—no—no! It was all real. Oh! that scream is in my ears still."

"I will convince you," said Aggie, taking my hand as she spoke. "Feel all along the verandah. Are the railings broken?"

I did as she bade me. No, though very wet, and clammy, the railing was intact!

"Where is the broken place?" she asked, imperatively.

Where, indeed?

"Now," she continued, "since you will not come in, look over, and you will see something more presently."

Shivering with fear, and the cold, drifting rain, I gazed down as she bade me, and there, far below, I saw lights moving rapidly to and fro, evidently in search of something. After a little delay they congregated in one place. There was a low, buzzing murmur—they had found him—and presently they commenced to ascend the hill, with the "hum-hum" of coolies carrying a burden. Nearer and nearer the lights and sounds came; up to the very brink of the khud, past the end of the verandah. Many steps and many torches—faint blue torches held by invisible hands—invisible but heavy-footed bearers carried their burden slowly upstairs, and along the passage and deposited it with a dump in Aggie's bedroom!

As we stood clasped in one another's arms, and shaking all over, the steps descended, the ghostly lights passed up the avenue, and gradually disappeared in the gathering darkness. The repetition of the tragedy was over for that day.

"Have you heard it before?" I asked with chattering teeth, as I bolted the drawing-room window.

"Yes, the evening of the picnic, and twice since. That is the reason I have always tried to stay out till late, and to keep you out. I was hoping and praying you might never hear it. It always happens just before dark: I am afraid you have thought me very queer of late. I have told no end of stories to keep you and the children from harm. I have—"

"I think you have been very kind," I interrupted. "Oh, Aggie, shall you ever get that crash, and that awful cry out of your head?"

"*Never!*" hastily lighting the caudles as she spoke.

"Is there anything more?" I inquired tremulously.

"Yes; sometimes at night, the most terrible weeping and sobbing in my bedroom;" and she shuddered at the mere recollection.

"Do the servants know?" I asked anxiously.

"The ayah Mumâ has heard it, and the khânsâ says his mother is sick, and he must go, and the bearer wants to attend his brother's wedding. They will *all* leave."

"I suppose most people know too?" I suggested dejectedly.

"Yes; don't you remember Mrs. Starkey's warnings, and her saying that without the verandah the house was worth double rent? We understand that dark speech of hers *now*, and we have not come to Cooper's Hotel yet."

"No, not *yet*. I wish we had. I wonder what Tom will say? He will be here in another fortnight. Oh, I wish he was here now!" In spite of our heart-shaking experience, we managed to eat, and drink, and sleep, yea, to play tennis—somewhat solemnly, it is true—and go to the club, where we remained to the very *last* moment; needless to mention, that I now entered into Aggie's *manoeuvre con amore*. Mrs. Starkey evidently divined the reason of our loitering in Kantia, and said in her most truculent manner, as she squared up to us—

"You keep your children out very late, Mrs. Shandon."

"Yes, but we like to have them with us," re-joined Aggie, in a meek apologetic voice.

"Then why don't you go home earlier?"

"Because it is so stupid, and lonely," was the mendacious answer.

"Lonely is not the word I should use. I wonder if you are as wise as your neighbours now? Come now, Mrs. Shandon."

"About what?" said Aggie, with ill-feigned innocence.

"About Briarwood. Haven't you heard it yet? The ghastly precipice and horse affair?"

"Yes, I suppose we may as well confess that we *have*."

"Humph! you are a brave couple to stay on. The Tombs tried it last year for three weeks. The Paxtons took it the year before, and then sub-let it; not that they believed in ghosts—oh, dear no!" and she laughed ironically.

"And what is the story?" I inquired eagerly.

"Well, the story is this. An old retired officer and his wife, and their pretty niece, lived at Briarwood a good many years ago. The girl was engaged to be married to a fine young fellow in the Guides. The day before the wedding, what you know of happened, and has happened every monsoon ever since. The poor girl went out of her mind, and destroyed herself, and the old colonel and his wife did not long survive her. The house is uninhabitable in the monsoon, and there seems nothing for it but to auction off the furniture, and pull it down; it will always be the same as long as it stands. Take *my* advice, and come into Cooper's Hotel. I believe you can have that small set of rooms at the back. The sitting-room smokes—but beggars can't be choosers."

"That will only be our very last resource," said Aggie, hotly.

"It's not very grand, I grant you but any port in a storm."

Tom arrived, was doubly welcome, and was charmed with Briarwood, chaffed us unmercifully, and derided our fears until *he* himself had a similar experience, and heard the phantom horse plunging in the verandah, and that wild, unearthly and utterly appalling shriek. No, he could not laugh *that* away; and seeing that we had now a mortal abhorrence of the place, that the children had to be kept abroad in the damp till long after dark, that Aggie was a mere hollow-eyed spectre, and that we had scarcely a servant left, that—in short, one day, we packed up precipitately and fled in a body to Cooper's Hotel. But we did not basely endeavour to sub-let, nor advertise Briarwood as "a delightfully situated pucka built house, containing all the requirements of a gentleman's family". No, no. Tom bore the loss of the rent, and—a more difficult feat—Aggie bore Mrs. Starkey's insufferable "I told you so."

Aggie was at Kantia again last season. She walked out early one morning to see our former abode. The chowkidar and parrot are still in possession, and are likely to remain the solo tenants on the premises. The parrot suns and dusts his ancient feathers in the empty verandah, which re-echoes with his cry of "Lucy, where are you—pretty Lucy?" The chowkidar inhabits a secluded go-down at the back, where he passes most of the day in sleeping, or smoking the soothing "hukka". The place has a forlorn, uncared-for appearance now; the flowers are nearly all gone; the paint has peeled off the doors and windows; the avenue is grass-grown. Briarwood appears to have resigned itself to emptiness, neglect, and decay, although outside the gate there still hangs a battered board, on which, if you look very closely, you can decipher the words *"To Let"*.

The North Verandah

A chance meeting in the hall of a Swiss hotel, in the vicinity of the visitors' book, a polite "After you", and a similarity of surnames led to our acquaintance with two charming Americans. The acquaintance ripened into friendship, and ultimately my sister Lucy and self discovered that Mrs. Washington-Dormer and her son Philip were connected with our family, and that we, the Dormers of Ashley Gardens, Victoria, London, S.W., were cousins (several times removed) of our namesakes of Rochelle, near Lexington, Kentucky, U.S.A.

Mrs. Dormer was a widow with a good figure, snow-white hair, and a bright, intelligent face. She had also a cheerful manner, and an air of suppressed energy. Having confessed to the national passion for old places, old curiosities and old pedigrees, she set to work to examine our family tree, from which it appeared that a certain relative had emigrated in the year 1810, settled, married and founded a dynasty in that State, so worthily celebrated for its thoroughbred horses and blue grass.

In company of "Cousin" Carolina and "Cousin" Philip, we travelled through Northern Italy and the Tyrol with mutual enjoyment, and before we separated in Paris had entered into a solemn league and covenant to visit our Kentucky cousins in the early "fall". I was rather astonished at the alacrity with which Lucy accepted this invitation—knowing that she was a hopelessly bad sailor and how she hated the sea! It, however, dawned on me that she liked Cousin Philip, and the least observant could see that he worshipped her.

Behold us therefore arrived and happily established at Rochelle, a stately old "colonial" house which, with its pillared verandahs on all four sides, presented a dignified appearance in the midst of spreading turf lawns (the beautiful blue grass), avenues of walnut trees, and clumps of oak and hickory.

In former days, Rochelle had been surrounded by an immense estate, worked by slaves who raised and gathered vast crops of hemp, tobacco, and corn; but now the shrunken acreage was chiefly devoted to the breeding and rearing of horses; for these Cousin Philip enjoyed a reputation that extended from New York to New Orleans. My sister Lucy was in her element, being a fearless rider and a capital whip; Cousin Carolina, too, was an admirable horsewoman, despite her fifty years. The days were spent in driving racing trotters, galloping young thorough-breds, visiting distant runs, and inspecting rival stables. These joys were not for *me!* I am naturally timid, a shameless coward where horses are concerned, distrustful of distant cows, and all strange dogs. I believe mine is what is termed "the artistic temperament" (I paint and write poetry), yet I have a certain queer courage of my own. For instance, I am not afraid to discharge a servant, to venture alone into a dark room, and have no belief in ghosts. When my sister, cousins, and their friends scoured the neighbourhood, I remained contentedly at Rochelle, sketching the best "bits" of scenery, the little black "piccaninnys", and the interior of the house itself. Mr. and Mrs. Gossett, Cousin Carolina's niece and nephew, were a gay young couple also of the party, which included Cousin Carolina's old schoolfellow, Miss Virginia Boone, a lineal descendant of the founder of the State. She was an interesting woman, and had a fund of stories relating to Kentucky and the Civil War, which rent the State in two. One day Lucy asked her to tell us something about Rochelle itself; it was so mellowed and solid, and in its way delightful, with an atmosphere of age and peace. Surely it had a history?

"Well, you see," said Miss Boone, clearing her throat, "Carolina has not lived here long—it's not *her* family place. It belonged to the Taylors a great while back, and it was standing empty for quite a spell. The grass is said to be the best in the world for young horses, and Philip was crazy to come here, so he routed his mother out at last; Rochelle was a dead bargain too, and though Carolina was loath to move, now she likes it." Then, as if to herself, she added, "She comes from a distance—or maybe she'd never have come at all!"

This was a dark saying, and I hastened to beg for some enlightenment.

Miss Boone seemed to hesitate before she answered rather vaguely, "Well, of course, all great plantations are the same."

"The same?" I echoed.

"Yes, where numbers of slaves have been employed. See," pointing to a row of lines or negro quarters to the north of the house. "I expect in Taylor's time there were hundreds there. The estates were some of the largest in Kentucky."

"Cousin Carolina still has black servants," I remarked.

"Oh yes—Uncle Pete, Mammy, and Jane were born in the family, the children of children, of slaves, yet devoted to the Dormers."

"Do you know, I saw such a forbidding looking nigger staring in through the breakfast-room window?" said Lucy. "I've never noticed him as one of the servants or hands, and he looked anything but devoted! He was coal black and big, and he pressed his hideous face close up against the glass door and scowled at me and muttered something; when I got up, and went to find out what he wanted, he was gone."

"A tramp," I suggested.

"Possibly. I hope I shan't see him again!" said Lucy, rising. "Here come the horses and the buggy; you," to me, "will have the house to yourself for the whole afternoon."

"So much the better," I answered; "I intend to make a sketch of Taffy, and there will be no one to distract his attention."

Taffy was a handsome fox-terrier, remarkable for a very short tail and great independence of character.

I watched the cavalcade turn down the avenue, Cousin Carolina and Miss Boone driving, followed by two mounted couples, and then set to work to persuade Taffy to sit for his portrait. By and by the fierce glare of the setting sun compelled me to retreat with my block, paint-box, and model into the north verandah. This overlooked from a respectful distance the servants' quarters—and, possibly for this reason, was but little frequented. It proved delightfully shady and almost empty, save for a few roomy old cane chairs, but now that I had obtained a satisfactory light my sitter began to fail me; he became restless, fidgety and disobedient, turning his head, pricking up his ears; finally he trotted off bodily. His attitude implied grave suspicion of something, or somebody—and his air was so uneasy that he almost gave the impression of there being an intruder in our vicinity—visible only to him!

This of course was a ridiculous idea, but as nothing would induce Taffy to "sit", I relinquished the hope of finishing my sketch, and fetching a book from the drawing-room, settled myself comfortably in one of the cane chairs and prepared to pass an hour of undisturbed enjoyment. The story of "Uncle Tom" proved to be absorbing; I had almost lost consciousness of my surroundings, when I was startled by a very peculiar sound quite close to me, a strange inarticulate gurgling noise, as if someone was being choked. I looked about; there was not a soul in the verandah, and I came to the conclusion that Taffy had swallowed a fly, which had gone the wrong way. I called to him; he was not fly-catching, but seemed to be staring intently at a certain closed door, and entirely unconscious of my presence.

I resumed my book, only to be again disturbed by this peculiar choking noise, and Taffy, with all his hair bristling on his back, now sought refuge under my chair, uttering low growls. At the same moment I noticed, coming directly from the servants' lines, a gigantic negro, whom I never remembered to have seen before. His head was bare, his face lowering and sullen; he wore a ragged blue and white stripped jacket, trousers turned up to his knees, and a pair of clumsy boots. As he advanced, with a deliberate, purposeful air, I became conscious of a sensation of fear, which increased with every stride.

The evening was still and warm, not a breath of air was stirring, the very leaves were motionless. Taffy was dumb, and the only sound to be heard was these doggedly approaching footsteps.

A door in the verandah was suddenly flung open and, to my amazement, there came forth a middle-aged lady, who was a complete stranger; she wore a flowing white dressing-gown, with wide sleeves; her reddish hair, of which she had a quantity, hung loosely to her waist, her figure was tall and slight, her sallow face—this I only saw in profile—looked hard as flint; the expression of her sharply-cut features was fiercely determined, and aggressive. She hurried across the verandah with light, pattering footsteps, and reached the railings that enclosed it, almost at the same moment as the huge black. I gathered that she addressed him angrily—her face expressed violent fury—but I could not distinguish a single word. I sat there motionless, an amazed and nervous spectator. Presently Taffy crawled out from under my chair, and with one piercing howl fled from the scene like a creature possessed.

I observed that the negro listened to his mistress with downcast eyes, and an air of stolid indifference, also that, as he waited, he held one hand against his back; grasped in that hand—invisible to the woman—was a shining blade about two feet long, which I recognised as the knife used for cane-cutting, and called a "machete".

As the two figures stood, one on the verandah, the other immediately beneath, I became aware that an enormous crowd had assembled outside the quarters, hundreds of coloured people—and a sudden hoarse hum arose, resembling the buzzing of angry bees. Finally the lady raised her clenched fist with a fierce, threatening gesture, and turned away.

As she did so, the negro gave a deep guttural laugh, reached out his arm, caught her violently by the hair, and dragged her head backwards over the edge of the railing. I saw her long thin throat, fully exposed, and it was with a shock of unexampled horror that I beheld the descent of a gleaming blade. With one swift stroke the wretched woman's head was severed from her body, and I heard the previous gurgling and choking sound, as it fell with a heavy thud upon the lawn, while the trunk collapsed in a hideous heap upon the boards of the verandah—which were instantly deluged with blood. The dreadful tide was flowing towards me, but I was unable to stir hand or foot—I felt as if I were paralysed.

As the murderer, stooping, lifted the head by its hair, I had a view of the blanched and ghastly face, and the wide-open eyes fixed in wild astonishment. He held it up towards the lines, and in response there rose strange, fierce, and prolonged yells of jubilation—such, I imagine, as are uttered by savages, when exulting over some fallen enemy. Then with his horrible trophy in one hand and a dripping knife in the other, the negro turned, and looked straight at *me*. Instantly everything became blurred, black darkness descended, and I remember no more!

When I came to myself, the clear imperative voice of Cousin Carolina was saying:

"My dear Marion, do you know that it is very imprudent to sleep out of doors at sundown—even in our exquisite climate?"

"Sleep!" I repeated, with an involuntary shudder; "I've not been sleeping," and with a painful effort I rose and tottered into a lighted sitting-room.

"What has happened to you, Marion?" cried my sister; "you look simply awful. Are you ill?—or have you seen a ghost?"

"Yes," I answered, looking round at six expectant faces, "I have seen *two* in the verandah!"

I noticed that Miss Boone gave me a quick, sharp look, but the rest of the company wore indulgent smiles, and Cousin Carolina said:

"No such thing as ghosts, my dear—it's only ignorant people like the negroes that believe in them *now*. You have Scotch blood in your veins, your mother was a Highlander, and no doubt you are a bit superstitious, and you have such imagination, dearest child, and are so highly strung. You have just dozed off and had a nightmare."

"Tell me, what do you think you saw?" enquired Philip, who had brought me a glass of wine.

I sipped this before I answered:

"A horrible sight, a lady in a white gown—I believe the owner of the estate—was beheaded in the verandah by a huge negro, and all the slaves—hundreds of them—shouted, and yelled for joy."

Mrs. Gossett, who was young and giddy, began to giggle, and then apologised, adding:

"It sounds so screamingly funny—a public execution in the Rochelle verandah!"

"It was just a bad nightmare, the combined result of crab salad at lunch, and *Uncle Tom's Cabin*," declared Cousin Carolina, "and nothing else. I believe there is a place—somewhere near Lexington—that *has* a story, but it is certainly not Rochelle, and sensible folk don't believe in such tales."

"No," I answered, now fortified by company and port wine. "But you will admit that seeing is believing. I've heard that my mother had second sight, and I'm afraid she has bequeathed it to *me*."

"My dear, you are a little upset," said Cousin Carolina; "don't think of your dream, and you will soon forget it. I daresay it was very vivid. I implore you not to repeat it to any of the servants, or we shall have the place in an uproar. Now just go and lie down, and get a rest before supper-time; Lucy will look after you. Another time, we won't leave you to keep house all alone."

Cousin Carolina was a despotic lady in her way, and would never suffer my nightmare in the back north verandah to be discussed. I still stuck to my opinion, but was as one to six—for even my own sister had deserted me and preached about imagination, and crab salad. It seemed impossible that a mere nightmare could ever be so vivid in its horror, and its realism. For several days I felt ill and nervous, and it was only my pride, Cousin Carolina's forcible character, and Mrs. Gossett's wild giggle, that restrained me from removing myself to an hotel at Lexington.

I never sat alone, and preferred a crowd to solitude. I even thrust my company on Phil and Lucy, now an engaged couple. Taffy and I were fast friends; we two had shared a unique experience—an experience apart. I was sensible of this bond in his manner, and I read it in the expression of his wistful and expressive eye.

A suspicion, nay, a conviction, took root in my mind. Miss Boone knew more about Rochelle than she pretended. More than once, I found her gazing at me, with an air of peculiar interest, and, more than once, curiosity had urged her to angle (very cautiously) for some particulars of the tragedy I thought I had seen; but I declined to indulge her. She was an unbeliever—and I held my tongue.

In the month of January, Lucy once more faced the Atlantic, accompanied by Miss Boone, Philip, and myself. She was obliged to arrange about her trousseau, and money affairs. We travelled by a big liner, and had on the whole a capital trip. Miss Boone found several friends among the passengers, and one afternoon as we sat in the library in the idle hour which follows tea, an old lady, her son and daughter joined our small circle. We discussed a variety of topics and impressions, and at last came to Kentucky State, Lexington, and Rochelle.

"Rochelle," repeated the lady's daughter. "Is not that the haunted house, Momma?"

"Yes, the Taylors' place," she answered briskly; "there is a dreadful story about it, but I fancy it is more or less forgotten by this time. For years and years it could not be let—the house, I mean; the land of course is most valuable."

"What is the story?" I enquired, and I glanced with some significance at Lucy and Philip.

"I remember hearing of it from my mother," continued the old lady, "and it's gospel truth. The Taylors were wealthy, and had a great estate, and hundreds of slaves, and were well thought of by all, till the time of Mrs. Herman Taylor, a widow, who inherited it from her husband. She was very strange—some said crazy—and lived alone; hoarded her money, flogged her slaves, and worked them to death. There were stories of terrible scenes at Rochelle—that lovely old place, so dignified and admired, had become a sort of negroes' hell! People could only talk—they did not dare to interfere. Marcella Taylor was a rich woman, and a vindictive enemy, and had over-seers as cruel and hard as herself, and she got more out of her slaves in the way of return than any mistress or master in the State. When it was moonlight, it was said, she worked them all night, and her crops were extraordinary.

At last the situation became intolerable; beyond the endurance of flesh and blood. A field hand who had been cruelly flogged took the law into his own hands, and one evening, in the sight of the entire community, executed Mrs. Taylor in her own verandah! He had been summoned to receive a punishment, and the story is, that he suddenly drew a long knife, which he had concealed, dragged her backwards by the hair, and beheaded her on the spot. He took the head with him, escaped to the woods, and was never seen or heard of again.

"It was also said that every anniversary the scene was re-enacted in the same verandah—but fortunately was only visible to some. The Villiers, who succeeded to the estates, hated the place, and got rid of it, and so for two generations the house has had a bad name, but now it is apparently recovering its character. I suppose the super-natural has a time-limit?"

She glanced at me interrogatively, but Miss Boone threw me an imploring look and I suffered silence to pass for assent. In this extraordinary and unexpected fashion my experience was confirmed, my truthfulness vindicated, there was an end to gibes about dreams, and crab salad. Subsequently Miss Boone confessed to me that the tale of the north verandah was not new to her, but that she had not wished to frighten Cousin Carolina. As if anything could frighten Cousin Carolina! She has nerves of cast-iron.

As for Lucy, she assured me with a rather unsteady laugh that when, as Mrs. Philip Dormer, she returned to Rochelle, nothing that could be offered would ever induce her to spend an afternoon there *alone*.

The First Comer

"Making night hideous." – Hamlet.

I am an old maid, and am not the least ashamed of the circumstance. Pray, why should women not be allowed the benefit of the doubt like men, and be supposed to remain single from choice?

I can assure you that it is not from want of *offers* that I am Miss Janet MacTavish, spinster. I could tell—but no matter. It is not to set down a list of proposals that I have taken pen in hand, but to relate a very mysterious occurrence that happened in our house last spring.

My sister Matilda and I are a well-to-do couple of maiden ladies, having no poor relatives, and a comfortable private fortune. We keep four servants (all female), and occupy a large detached house in a fashionable part of Edinburgh, and the circle in which we move is most exclusive and genteel.

Matilda is a good deal older than I am (though we dress alike), and is somewhat of an invalid.

Our east winds are certainly trying, and last March she had a very sharp attack of bronchitis, brought on (between ourselves) by her own rash imprudence. Though I may not say this to her face, I may say it here.

She does not approve of fiction, though, goodness knows, what I am going to set down is not fiction, but fact; but any literary work in a gay paper cover (of course,

127

I don't mean tracts), such as novels and magazines, is an abomination in her eyes, and "reading such-like trash" she considers sinful waste of time.

So, even if this falls into her hands by an odd chance, she will never read it, and I am quite safe in writing out everything that happened, as I dare not do if I thought that Mattie was coming after me and picking holes in every sentence.

Matilda is terribly particular about grammar and orthography, and reads over all my letters before I venture to close them.

Dear me, how I have wandered away from my point! I'm sure that no one will care to know that I am a little in awe of my elder, that she treats me sometimes as if I were still in my teens. But people may like to hear of the queer thing that happened to me, and I am really and truly coming to it at last.

Matilda was ill with bronchitis, very ill. Bella (that's our sewing-maid and general factotum, who has been with us twelve years this term) and I took it in turns to sit up with her at night. It happened to be my night, and I was sitting over the fire in a half-kind of doze, when Matilda woke up, and nothing would serve her but a cup of tea of all things, at two o'clock in the morning—the kitchen fire out, no hot water, and every one in the house in their beds, except myself.

I had some nice beef-tea in a little pan beside the hob, and I coaxed her hard to try some of that, but not a bit of it. Nothing would serve her but real tea, and I knew that once she had taken the notion in her head, I might just as well do her bidding first as last. So I opened the door and went out, thinking to take the small lamp, for, of course, all the gas was out, and turned off at the meter—as it ought to be in every decent house.

"You'll no do that!" she said, quite cross. Mattie speaks broad when she is vexed, and we had had a bit of argument about the tea. "You'll no do that, and leave me here without the light! Just go down and infuse me a cup of tea as quick as ever you can, for I know I'll be awfully the better of it!"

So there was just nothing else for it, and down I went in the pitch-black darkness, not liking the job at all.

It was not that I was afraid. Not I. But the notion of having to rake up and make the kitchen fire, and boil the kettle, was an errand that went rather against the grain, especially as I'm a terrible bad hand at lighting a fire.

I was thinking of this and wondering where were the wood and the matches to be found, when, just as I reached the head of the stairs, I was delighted to hear a great raking out of cinders below in the kitchen. Such a raking and poking and banging of coals and knocking about of the range I never did hear, and I said to myself—

"This is fine; it's washing morning" (we do our washing at home) "and later than I thought; and the servants are up, so it's all right;" and I ran down the kitchen stairs, quite inspirited like by the idea. As I passed the door of the servants' room (where cook and housemaid slept), Harris, that's the housemaid, called out—

"Who's that?"

I went to the door and said—

"It's I, Miss Janet. I want a cup of tea for Miss MacTavish."

In a moment Harris had thrown on some clothes and was out in the passage. She was always a quick, willing girl, and very obliging. She said (it was black dark, and I could not see her)—

"Never you mind. Miss Janet; I'll light the fire and boil up the kettle in no time."

"You need not do that," said I, "for there's some one at the fire already—cook, I suppose."

"Not me, ma'am" said a sleepy voice from the interior of the bedroom. "I'm in my bed."

"Then who can it be?" I asked, for the banging and raking had become still more tremendous, and the thunder of the poker was just awful!

"It must be Bella," said Harris, feeling her way to the kitchen door and pushing it open, followed by me.

We stood for full half a minute in the dark, whilst she felt about and groped for the matches, and still the noise continued.

"Bella," I said crossly, "what on earth—"

But at this instant the match was struck, and dimly lit up the kitchen. I strained my eyes into the darkness, whilst Harris composedly lit a candle. I looked, and looked, and looked again, but there was no one in the kitchen but ourselves.

I was just petrified, I can tell you, and I staggered against the dresser, and gaped at the now silent fireplace. The coals and cinders and ashes were exactly as they had gone out, not a bit disturbed; any one could see that they had never been stirred.

"In the name of goodness, Harris," I said in a whisper, "where is the person that was poking that fire? You heard them yourself!"

"I heard a noise, sure enough, Miss Janet," she said, not a bit daunted; "and if I was a body that believed in ghosts and such-like clavers, I'd say it was them," putting firewood in the grate as she spoke. "It's queer, certainly. Miss MacTavish will be wearying for her tea," she added. "I know well what it is to have a kind of longing for a good cup. Save us! what a cold air there is in this kitchen. I wonder where cook put the bellows."

Seeing that Harris was taking the matter so coolly, for very shame I was forced to do the like; so I did not say a word about my misgivings, nor the odd queer thrill I had felt as we stood in the pitch darkness and listened to the furious raking of the kitchen grate.

How icy cold the kitchen had been! just like a vault, and with the same damp, earthy smell!

I was in a mighty hurry to get back upstairs, believe me, and did all in my power to speed the fire and the kettle, and in due time we wended our way above, Harris bearing the tea on a tray, and walking last.

I left her to administer the refreshment, whilst I went into Bella's room, which was close by, candle in hand.

"You are awake, I see, Bella," I remarked, putting it down as I spoke (I felt that I must unbosom myself to some one, or never close an eye that night). "Tell me, did you hear a great raking of the kitchen fire just now?"

"Yes, miss, of course. Why, it woke me. I suppose you had occasion to go down for something, Miss Janet; but why did you not call me?"

"It was not I who woke you, Bella," I rejoined quickly. "I was on my way downstairs when I heard that noise below, and I thought it was cook or Harris, but when I got down Harris came out of the bedroom. Cook was in bed. Maggie, you know, is up above you, and we went into the kitchen, thinking it might be you or her, and lit a candle; but I give you my word of honour that, although the noise was really terrible till we struck a light, when we looked about us not a soul was to be seen!"

At this, Bella started up in bed, and became of a livid, chalky kind of colour.

"No one. Miss Janet?" she gasped out.

"Not a soul!" I replied solemnly.

"Then, oh!" she exclaimed, now jumping bodily out on the floor, and looking quite wild and distracted, "tell me, in Heaven's name, which of you went into the kitchen first, you or Harris?" She was so agitated, she seemed scarcely able to bring out the words, and her eyes rested upon mine with a strange, frightened look, that made me fancy she had taken temporary leave of her wits.

131

"Harris went first" I answered shortly.

"Thank Heaven for that!" she returned, now collapsing on the edge of her bed. "But poor Kate Harris is a dead woman!"

I stared hard at Bella, as well I might. Was she talking in her sleep? or was I dreaming?

"What do you mean, Bella Cameron?" I cried. "Are you gone crazy? Are you gone clean daft?"

"It was a warning," she replied, in a low and awe-struck voice. "We Highlanders understand the like well! It was a warning of death! Kate Harris's hour has come."

"If you are going to talk such wicked nonsense, Bella" I said, "I'm not going to stop to listen. Whatever you do, don't let Matilda hear you going on with such foolishness. The house would not hold her, and you know that well."

"All right, Miss Janet; you heard the commotion your-self—you will allow that; and you will see that the kitchen grate is never raked out for nothing. I only wish, from the bottom of my heart, that what I've told you may not come true; but, bad as it was, I'm thankful that you were not first in the kitchen."

A few more indignant expostulations on my part, and lamentations on Bella's, and then I went back to Matilda, and it being now near three o'clock, and she inclined to be drowsy, I lay down on the sofa, and got a couple of hours' sleep.

A day or two afterwards I was suddenly struck with a strange thrill of apprehension by noticing how very, very ill Kate Harris looked. I taxed her with not feeling well, and she admitted that she had not been herself, and could not say what ailed her. She had no actual pain, but she felt weak all over, and could scarcely drag herself about the house: "It would go off. She would not see a doctor—No, no, no!—It was only just a kind of cold feeling in her bones, and a sort of notion that a hand was gripping her throat. It was all fancy; and Dr. Henderson (our doctor) would make fine game of her if he saw her by way of being a patient. She would be all right in a day or two." Vain hope! In a day or two she was much worse. She was obliged to give in—to take to her bed. I sent for Dr. Henderson—indeed he called daily to visit Mattie—so I had only to pilot him down below to see Kate. He came out to me presently with a very grave face, and said—

"Has she any friends?"—pointing towards Kate's door with his thumb.

"Friends! To be sure," I answered. "She has a sister married to a tram conductor in Wickham Street."

"Send for her at once; and you had better have her moved. She can't last a week."

"Do you mean that she is going to die?" I gasped, clutching the balusters, for we were standing in the lower hall.

"I am sorry to say the case is hopeless. Nothing can save her, and the sooner she is with her own people the better."

I was, I need scarcely tell you, greatly shocked—terribly shocked—and presently, when I had recovered myself, I sent off, post-haste, for Kate's sister.

I went in to see her. She, poor creature, was all curiosity to know what the doctor had said.

"He would tell me nothing, miss," she observed smilingly. "Only felt my pulse, and tried my heart with a stethoscope, and my temperature with that queer little tube. I only feel a bit tired and out of breath; but you'll find I'll be all right in a day or two. I'm only sorry I'm giving all this trouble, and Bella and Mary having to do my work. However, I'll be fit to clean the plate on Saturday."

Poor soul, little did she dream that her work in this world was done!

And I, as I sat beside the bed and looked at her always pale face, her now livid lips and hollow eyes, told myself that already I could see the hand of Death on her countenance. I was obliged to tell her sister what the doctor had said; and how she cried—and so did I—and who was to tell Kate? We wished to keep her with us undisturbed—Matilda and I—but her people would not hear of it, and so we had an ambulance from the hospital and sent her home.

She just lived a week, and, strange to say, she had always the greatest craving for me to be with her, for me to sit beside her, and read to her, and hold her hand. She showed far more anxiety for *my* company than for that of any of her own people.

Bella alone, of all the household, expressed no astonishment when she heard the doctor's startling verdict. Being in Mattie's room at the time, she merely looked over at me gravely, and significantly shook her head.

One evening Bella and I were with her; she had lain silent for a long time, and then she said to me quite suddenly

"Miss Janet, you'll remember the morning you came downstairs looking for Miss MacTavish's tea?" (Did I not recollect it, only too well!) "Somehow, I got a queer kind of chill then; I felt it at the time, to the very marrow of my bones. I have never been warm since. It was just this day fortnight. I remember it well, because it was washing Monday."

That night Kate Harris died. She passed away, as it were, in her sleep, with her hand in mine. As she was with me on that mysterious night, so I was now with her.

Call me a superstitious old imbecile, or what you like, but I firmly believe that, had I entered that kitchen first, it would have been Janet MacTavish, and not Kate Harris, who was lying in her coffin!

Of course Matilda knows nothing of this, nor ever will. Perhaps—for she is one of your strong-minded folk—she would scout at the idea, and at me, for a daft, silly body, and try to explain it all away quite reasonable like. I only wish she could!

Trooper Thompson's Information

"Foul deeds will rise,
Though all the earth o'erwhelm them, to men's eyes"

– Hamlet.

Thirty years ago, when Australia was not the camping ground it is now. I was a trooper in the mounted police. I had gone out to the goldfields, like thousands of other younger sons, expecting to make my fortune; my expectations, however, were not fulfilled—far from it! On the contrary, as in the case of the dog and the shadow, I lost all the substance I possessed.

After toiling for months in a worn-out claim, often knee-deep in water, my chum bolted with our pitiful accumulation of gold-dust; and a pick, cradle, and the clothes I stood in represented my worldly all. Under these distressing circumstances, I was thankful to enlist in the mounted police. The reputation of being pretty steady, and a good man on a horse, were my sole credentials.

The pay was small; I was a long way astray from the pleasant high-road which leads to fortune. Work was incessant, and promotion slow. I had been nearly three years in the force, and was still Trooper Thompson, and began to fear that as Trooper Thompson I should live and die, when that well-known tide which interferes so potently in the affairs of men set my way at last!

We had been out for two days on the track of a party of notorious bushrangers, and returned empty-handed to our headquarters, pretty done up, to find, when all stragglers were assembled, that Trooper Martin was missing. Just before dark his bay mare galloped in, covered with dust and sweat; but all her accoutrements were complete, and there was not a speck of blood on saddle or holsters, nor anything about her to afford the faintest clue to the fate or whereabouts of the rider. Had he met with foul play? Had the mare broken away, and left him on for to lose himself and perish in the trackless bush?

A rigorous search was instituted at sunrise—a search that was repeated for five days; not a perch of ground was left unexplored within a radius of ten miles, nevertheless this indefatigable quest proved unavailing. Martin, one of the smartest of our men, appeared to have been as completely lost as if the earth had opened her mouth and swallowed him up, like Korah, Dathan, and Abiram

None so keen and so eager over the pursuit of Martin as our chief; none so irritable and impatient at the futile result of his tireless exertions. However, he was compelled to leave our headquarters for a week on urgent business in another quarter of the district; and before he set out, he sent for me and spoke to me privately,

"Look here, Thompson," he said, you have a fairly good head on your shoulders; use your wits, and find out what has become of our man. If you succeed, I promise you promotion—and mind this, I shall expect to hear of Martin, dead or alive, when I return this day week, so, be up and doing."

I saluted, and muttered that I would do my best, but inwardly asked myself how I could hope to succeed, when one of the most experienced officers had failed? And yet I might by chance stumble on some clue!

I puzzled over the matter day and night; and I can conscientiously affirm that, whether I rode about the neighbouring sheep-runs, scoured the bush, dragged water-holes, or lay tossing on my cot, Martin was never out of my thoughts.

Three of the precious days had gone by—had flown—and yet no trace of our missing comrade, work, ponder, track as I would. At length it came to the eve of the chief's return, and, alas! I was no nearer promotion than when he had started, though I had covered miles of country and lost whole nights of sleep. I was utterly worn out with my fruitless quest that evening, and after a hasty meal threw myself on my cot, and slept the sleep of utter exhaustion. I cannot say how long this sleep may have lasted, but the moon was shining full into the window when I was awoke by someone in heavy boots entering my room—a man—who came over and stood at the foot of my bed; and I must confess that I was a good deal startled when I recognised Martin.

"Hullo!" I shouted, "where the dickens have you been? Why did you not report yourself?"

No reply—but Ned Martin was always slow of speech.

"A pretty fright you have given us—and a nice search we have had!"

I sat up and stared hard at my comrade, and noticed that he looked white and death-like. His eyes as they met mine had a strange lack-lustre expression—no doubt the poor chap had been nearly starved in the bush.

"What's up?" I asked impatiently; "why the devil can't you speak?"

Martin was always a silent chap, but to stand gazing at me and never opening his mouth, after a ten-days' leave of absence, was rather too much.

At last he answered in a low husky voice, that sounded as if it were far away.

"Ten miles west—Laffan's Run—Shepherd's Hut—six yards to rear—six feet deep."

Then he suddenly turned round, and made for the door. As I jumped out of bed and hurried after him, I noticed by the searching moonlight that there was a great black stain on the back of his coat, just below the left shoulder. He crossed the kitchen and went out, I still following him, calling after him to "wait", to "hold hard"; but even as I stood on the threshold he was gone—where? where?

Gaze as I would, there was not a soul to be seen, not a living thing—nothing but the cold weird moonlight, illuminating a vast expanse of plain, and a few scraggy blue gum trees. A sudden, inexplicable chill seized me! I closed and bolted the door with palsied precipitation and ran back to bed, and—yes, truth is best—covered my head up with the clothes and lay in a cold sweat for what seemed to me days, my heart thumping like a steam-hammer, I had seen—a ghost.

I struggled madly with an overwhelming sense of horror, but by degrees this feeling wore off. Had it not been a bad dream—a nightmare—that I would have forgotten by dawn? Compelled by some strange instigation I crawled timidly out of bed, lit a candle, and wrote down—"Ten miles west; Laffan's Run, Shepherd's Hut, six yards to rear, six feet deep", and then crept back between the blankets, where I lay sweltering between fear and indecision. If it was a dream, what a pretty fool I should look if I took the men out on a ten-miles' wild-goose chase and "stuck up" an innocent individual! Instead of promotion, I ran a fairly good chance of being dismissed from the force in disgrace.

At one moment I resolved to have nothing to do with the vision, at another I decided to follow Martin's directions and to stand my chance. Finally I fell asleep, determined to take no steps whatever in the matter; yet, even as I dozed, an indefinable something continually urged me to go to Laffan's Run—a shuddering whisper seemed to say, "Here is your opportunity at last; seize it."

After hours of miserable hesitation, I roused the men, but I took no one into my confidence—it was surely another voice than mine which boldly addressed my amazed comrades.

"Prepare to start for Laffan's Run in half an hour. Take a spare horse—Martin's mare will do—a piece of rope, a pair of handcuffs, and a couple of spades."

As a matter of course, I was a good deal chaffed, but received all witticisms within inflexible composure,

"You seem very sure of your bird, boss? Did you get the hint by telegram? I suppose Martin is expecting us to breakfast?"

These and similar remarks were made, to all of which I turned a stolid countenance and a deaf ear. To tell the truth, I was very far from confident, and though I led the party with much assurance, and at a sharp canter, my heart was thumping fast, and beads of perspiration broke out upon my face. On the result of the next hour's developments depended my whole future. I should either be infallibly branded as an incapable and mischievous idiot, or I should be known far and wide as one of the cleverest detective officers in West Australia. Which would be?

It was barely seven o'clock when we surrounded the hut—the hut I had been desired to seek. Laffan's shepherd was a ticket-of-leave, who had been several years on the station. His name was Henderson: a man with a somewhat villainous expression, an impediment in his speech, and a very powerful frame. He was stooping over the fire, engrossed in frying a bit of mutton for his breakfast, when I entered, followed by four troopers.

"Hullo!" he stammered, looking back over his shoulder. "What's up? What you want here?"

"I want you!" I answered promptly. "I arrest you," producing the handcuffs, "for the murder of Trooper Martin."

He turned on me fiercely, almost ere I had ceased speaking, and dashed the frying-pan in my face.

"Handcuff him," I said,

"Handcuff me!" struggling like a wild beast. "And for what? Where's your proof?" he stuttered. "I swear I never saw Martin since Christmas. You'll suffer for this—rot for it—swing for it," he screamed, when the bracelets were locked. "What you mean by 'sticking up' an innocent man, eh? Just wait till Laffan and your boss hear of it. What do I know of Martin?" he asked, with a string of rare and blood-curdling oaths. "What are ye going on?" he yelled.

I was going, recklessly and trustfully, on information received from a spirit; and I felt desperately nervous as I gave the order for two troopers to hobble horses and fetch spades. Meanwhile I measured with shaking hands six good yards from the back of the hut, and desired the men to set to work on the ground immediately.

The soil was loose—a suspicious and, to me, encouraging sign—nevertheless, the job was by no means an easy one. When the men had dug down to a depth of five feet, I shook as if with ague whilst each spadeful was thrown up on the grass, and as yet there was no sign.

Suddenly one of the diggers shouted—

"By gum! there's a body here!"

"And a trooper's boot," added his comrades excitedly.

They now made a frenzied spurt, and presently called out with one breath, "It's Martin!" Then alternately, "He's been done for"—"He is dead"—"this ten days."

Yes, there was no doubt whatever of his identity. It was the missing man, and my reputation was saved. Poor Ned Martin! He had been treacherously stabbed in the back, and buried as he fell.

I called to the troopers within doors to bring out the prisoner. At first I believe he struggled violently, but ultimately submitted to be conducted to where he had interred his victim. He stood motionless, and looked down into the grave; then he slowly raised his eyes and fastened them on me.

"Blast you!" he stammered, in a low, choked voice. "How did you know? Who told you?"

"Never you mind who; that's my business."

"But not a soul saw it—not even the dog. I had an old grudge against that hound there."

"Mind, I caution you against saying anything that may be used against you," I said. "You had better hold your tongue."

"Hold my tongue! And to what good, when I'll have to swing for him? He said so. Yes, that's his revolver; I had not the heart to bury it—it's a beauty. But if I had my wrists free, and it in my hand, I'd drill a few holes in some of you! Listen! Martin he come in to light his pipe, and as he stooped over the fire I stabbed him with a butcher's knife right under the shoulder-blade. It was a mortal wound; he only said, 'You'll swing for this,' and 'Mother!' Then the blood choked him. After that he give up the ghost, and I dragged him out by the heel, and buried him as you see. You chaps have been round pretty often, and never smoked a case! No human eye saw—I took good care to leave no trace. I loosed his mare four miles from here—and how you know is a miracle. How did you find out?"

I shook my head.

"Maybe he told. He used to come of a night, and peer in at the window, and the dog would howl awful, and hide. Folks as has been put away has no business to walk."

We buried Martin where we had found him, then mounted Henderson on his mare, and brought him handcuffed to the head station. We also fetched away the dog. Our party reached quarters almost simultaneously with the arrival of the chief, and to him I formally made over my prisoner.

The chief was delighted at my success, and overwhelmed me with compliments; but although I have hitherto never divulged the truth, I here frankly confess that I owe praise, promotion, and all my subsequent notoriety to the reliable information which I received from Trooper Martin's Ghost.

Who Knew the Truth?

our years ago my sister Ursula reversed the fashion of the day, and married a wealthy young American, George P. Forrest, of Forrest & Sons, Bullion Buildings, Broadway; and, as a natural consequence, this alliance led to some intimacy between two hitherto unfamiliar circles, as well as a considerable outlay in tickets on the Atlantic liners

George and Ursie visited her old home every "fall", and on the conclusion of their last Europe tour they insisted on carrying me back with them across the "herring pond", in order to introduce me to the New World.

As Ursula's eldest and favourite brother, an extremely kind reception was accorded me by her friends—especially her girl friends. We had a very gay season in New York, which I thoroughly enjoyed, but the end of three months' dancing, dining out, driving, and skating, found me somewhat fagged, and I gladly hailed George's announcement that he was going to take me right away "down South", to the part of the world which had been the home of his ancestors.

"I know a whole crowd of folk who will be glad to put us up, and give us a real good time," he said. "Are you for coming?"

I assured him that I was ready to start at an hour's notice.

"South Carolina is our State, you see; my father was raised there. He was in Charleston in blockade days. Poor old Charleston, the grass is growing in her streets now."

We set out on our journey, a party of four—George and I, his cousin Edward Stewart, and a rich financier called Van Boom.

To me this expedition was a totally new experience. The wonderful southern vegetation, the fine old houses (once belonging to Royalist families), which combined the stateliness of English mansions, with the easy luxury of the tropics, above all the hospitality of the inmates, afforded an almost startling surprise. If I ever return to America, I shall pitch my tent in South Carolina.

We had nearly come to the end of our trip, when the following curious experience befell me.

One afternoon we had been wading through the soft marshy ground in the rice fields after snipe. Our bag was seventy brace, we were twelve miles from our headquarters and the heat was overpowering, when Van Boom gave out. He was a stout-short-necked, self-indulgent millionaire, who had accompanied us for a "cure".

"It's no manner of good," he declared. "It's all very well for you Britishers, who have no occupation and nothing to do but shoot and fox-hunt; but I'm not used to this sort of work. You'll have to go on and leave me. It's either that or *carry* me! I can't sit my horse any longer."

We had an imposing following of chattering blacks, and, having explained the situation to them, a young mulatto, pointing to a long line of trees in the distance, said: "Very good house still, everything same as in old massa's time, they say. Best stop here."

To this suggestion a white-haired veteran objected, but was silenced by the young man, who had now installed himself as our pioneer.

In ten minutes' time we had arrived before the sunken piers of what had once been a fine gateway, leading to a long majestic avenue of walnut-trees. The avenue was grass-grown, and at the far end loomed an unexpected sight—a stately white mansion of commanding appearance. As we approached nearer, we realised that it was surrounded by decaying pillared verandahs, a wild overgrown pleasure ground, clumps of live oaks, and the "tender grace of a day that is dead".

Even the very steps were grass-grown—though the door stood wide. Sitting upon the threshold was a fat negress, with a bright orange bandana tied round her head, engaged in manufacturing what looked like a pink ball dress. In the background were several dusky piccaninnies, and a shrivelled old man.

Our mulatto guide immediately strutted forward and volubly explained our predicament, whilst we surveyed the residence—a solidly-built three-storeyed square house, invaded on all sides by a wild tangle of magnolias, or-ange-trees, palms, dense masses of pomegranate and lemon plant—wondering at its romantic and poetic desolation, its forlorn and deserted appearance.

After a scene of considerable altercation and hesitation, we were invited to dismount; our horses were led away, and we entered a great square hall surrounded by a gallery, from which looked down the pictured faces of dead-and-gone owners of the old house residence.

The light seemed dim after the outside glare, and the coolness of the atmosphere, to our sun-scorched frames, struck like the interior of a tomb.

The fat, gay negress was both loquacious and hospitable. She was also a capable creature; the piccaninnies were sent flying on various errands, not unconnected with the com-missariat, and we were formally conducted upstairs, and requested to make a selection of apartments.

That there should be so many available bedrooms was a distinct surprise. Van Boom, like the millionaire he was, selected, as his due, the best; I, as a stranger in the land, was

145

requested to make second choice. I chose a large chamber with two big windows overlooking the avenue. Its four-post bed and open fireplace reminded me of home, which, I believe, was the sole reason that I preferred it.

In one corner stood an old secretaire, priceless to a collector of antique furniture, the stiff, high-backed chairs were to match, and over the chimney-piece hung a large Scriptural print in a heavy black frame, representing "The Death of Jehu"; underneath was inscribed: "Had Jehu peace who slew his master?" The window curtains were of faded chintz, and the floor was dark polished oak, in places almost black.

I flung open a window, and gazed down the great avenue. The air of the room was close and musty (indeed, the entire mansion was pervaded with that peculiar and melancholy odour known as "dry rot"). As I leant my elbow on the sill, I inhaled the penetrating perfume of magnolia and jasmin; my eyes rested on dense masses of laurels, palmettos, myrtle, and orange trees. In the distance was the wide expanse of rich savannahs, melting into vivid green rice fields, which, in their turn, faded away in the soft blue horizon.

What a delicious, peaceful spot! As I stood by the window, I seemed to fall under the influence of the languor and dreaminess of the South, and to feel its subtle charm.

The spell was abruptly broken by the loud, full voice of a stalwart black, hurrying down the avenue with a basket on his head, singing as he went; and the words of his song which floated up to me, were these:

Oh, shout, shout, de deb'l is about;
Oh, shut yo' do' an' keep him out,
I don' want to stay here no longer.
For he is so much like a snaky in de grass,
Ef you don' mind, he will get you at las',
I don' want to stay her no longer.

From the far end of the avenue came back the refrain, now growing gradually fainter—

Shout . . . shout . . . de deb'l is about;

and I turned, startled by a slight movement in the room, to find an old man entering with a great can of water; as his eyes met mine he shook his head, saying:

"I very sorry massa take dis room."

"Why?" I asked.

He made no reply beyond a more solemn shaking of his head, accompanied by a lamentable groan, and a call, that dinner was ready, hurried me below.

The bustling negress and her staff had served up an excellent meal of boiled fowl, with rice, roast snipe, and banana fritters. These were succeeded by fruit from the old garden, and unexpectedly good black coffee.

A sufficient supply of plate, glass, and crockery was forthcoming, and, on our expressing our amazement at such luxuries, the negress replied:

"House belong to our massa—he live in Europe—never come here—but all ready."

After dinner we sat for some time on the verandah watching a red, red moon rise above the rice fields; whilst the fragrance of the flower-scented air, the deep stillness of the night, and the soft, enervating atmosphere, seemed to steal its way into one's very soul.

At last George sprang to his feet, and exclaimed:

"I say! don't let us fall asleep yet; come round and see the horses—they are away back somewhere."

After a short walk we found our steeds installed and picketed in what had once been a rose garden, and comfortably located for the night. A good many peering dusky faces watched us as we strolled past the roofless stables, and the long lines of half-deserted cabins. As we were returning George said to me: "This is one of those old places abandoned and left to go to wrack and ruin because the owners prefer to live elsewhere, or they are broke, or er—er—because something has happened here."

"Not much could happen *here*," cried Van Boom, now restored by rest and food; "it's such a drowsy sort of abode, one feels half asleep."

"It's a lovely, picturesque old spot," remarked Edward Stewart, "but I don't say I should like to live here altogether. However, I'm glad I've seen it, and I shall often revisit this old plantation in my dreams. I wonder what is its history."

"I can give a good guess at that," rejoined George. "An old Royalist family in the style of Thackeray's *Virginians*, built this house, kept state and slaves, cut a great figure in wig-and-hoop days. Were badly knocked about by the war—income diminished, slaves enfranchised; possibly came down to one old man, the last of his race—property goes to distant branch. Fresh start."

Van Boom blew the smoke through his nostrils, and snorted. "Not much sign of a fresh start *here*, not the sort of place I should care to revisit in *my* dreams; but I'm going to dream now. Goodnight"; and he stalked housewards, whither we followed him in single file.

I happened to be the one to bring up the rear, for I lagged behind enjoying the beautiful tropical night. The moon rode high in the deep violet heavens, and, as I passed a thicket of magnolias, it seemed to me that among the white blossoms there peered forth a black malignant face. I looked away for a moment, then glanced back . . . it was gone! What tricks imagination does play! We hear of faces in the fire—this had been a face among the flowers!

When I at last entered the hall, I found my companions had already retired to bed. A toothless old negress brought me a candle, and informed me that we were alone in the house, as she and the other blacks slept in the so-called "lines" at the back of the premises.

Although the night was warm, I was agreeably surprised (remembering the cold chill of the room) to find that a large wood fire had been lit, and was blazing cheerfully up the chimney, illuminating the whole scene. The light caught the lower part of the gloomy print, and threw out in grim relief: "Had Jehu peace who slew his master?"

Outside the moon shone full over moss and thicket, on lily, magnolia, and live oaks, and, as I cannot sleep in a strong light, I drew the shabby window-curtains before I subsided under the canopy of the four-poster. I was very tired. Wading knee-deep in the treacherous ooze of a rice swamp is rather different to striding through the heather, or breasting a brae on a Scottish moor, and I was soon asleep, undisturbed by the hoarse and clamorous croaking of the frogs in the marsh.

I must have been asleep for a considerable time, when, half between sleeping and waking, I was aware of a curious noise—a soft, monotonous, repeated knocking, which became so continuous and distinct that I was soon thoroughly aroused, and, by the still bright light of the fire, was not a little astonished to behold the empty rocking-chair, in vigorous motion!

I stared and stared—and yet it rocked and rocked, as if occupied by someone who was equally energetic and impatient. I had heard of table-turning—here was a chair moving, and there was something uncanny about its insolent indifference to *me*. Presently the chair creaked and was jerked back—the sitter had evidently risen.

With deliberate heavy footsteps he (for it was surely a man!) walked to the window; meanwhile I was sitting up in bed, anxiously awaiting further developments.

The tattered curtains were now brusquely drawn aside, the lattice of the window was opened, and I knew instinctively that something was standing there—gazing down the avenue.

For a long time there was an expressive silence, at length disturbed by a sort of irritated tapping on the window-sill—as if the watcher were waiting for something and his patience was becoming exhausted.

And, strange to say, it was chiefly this irritated tapping that impressed me with a sensation of horror, and recalled to my mind the gruesome "Death Watch". Suddenly the sound ceased, and, after listening with all my faculties strung to the highest pitch of anticipation, I lay down again.

By-and-by my heart gave a violent jerk, as the solid, slow steps went from the window to the door, and an invisible hand shot the bolt with murderous emphasis.

Another silence—the thing moved towards the old bureau, and I heard the clink! clink! of coin; presently I was aware of loud breathing beside me, and conscious of stealthy touches fingering the bedclothes—of a cautious fumbling with the coverlet, and *then* suddenly, with a force that made my heart leap—an enormous hand was on my mouth! Before I could move its fellow had seized my throat with the grip of a steel trap. I struggled fiercely and with all my strength; I flung my arms out, but of what use was my feeble resistance? The air was empty! Yet the terrible hand never once relaxed its hold—my life seemed to ebb away from me . . . I was . . . dying—I was sensible that I was in the clutch of Death!

And now I began to realise that I was about to be taken away and buried. My limp and lifeless body was thrust into what I supposed was a sack—the bolt was withdrawn—I was hauled across the gallery, and down the stairs with a bump, bump, bump—then out of the house into the garden, and dragged through the high, wet grasses, bruising in my passage the scented wild geranium, whose crushed stalks gave out a pungent odour (I shudder at the smell of scented geraniums to this day!)—through clumps of magnolias and an atmosphere sickly with their heavy perfume.

Presumably it was a hot night; and yet the blood in my veins ran ice. Death was taking me to a nameless grave.

At last my gruesome journey was ended, and the sole noises that fell on my ears was the thud of a working spade. The digging ceased, the task was evidently complete; slow footsteps came towards me . . . then . . . I heard no more.

It was broad daylight when I awoke. I sat up in bed wondering if my experience of the past night had been a dream! The birds were singing, someone was thrumming a banjo; and a soft white mist was rising over the rice fields. Yes—no doubt it was a hideous nightmare; but who, or what, had drawn aside the curtains?

My head ached abominably. I felt feverish; anything but refreshed after a long night's rest. The face that confronted me in the looking-glass was haggard and hollow-eyed, and I noticed deep red traces of finger marks on my throat! And even as I looked—they faded.

My somewhat shattered appearance was promptly remarked on at breakfast; I attributed the cause to "a touch of fever" (a useful explanation that has done gallant service), and my excuse was accepted without demur.

After a particularly hearty breakfast, Van Boom declared himself quite fit for his twelve-mile ride, and while George was distributing bucksheesh to the servants, I strolled out into the abandoned garden.

Was it solely its luxuriance of oleanders, stephanotis, orange flowers, this tangled jungle of exquisite free flowers, that had such an extraordinary fascination for me? or was it possible that I was looking for my own grave?

Whilst I stood wondering and speculating, I caught sight of the old man, and beckoned to him.

As he approached, he looked at me with a curious expression of interrogation in his prominent brown eyes.

"Tell me, uncle, what is the story of the room I slept in last night?"

"No story, massa," rolling his eyes at me. "No story—no story!"

"Come," I said, "think again, Uncle Tom."

But he merely wagged his head in hopeless ignorance.

"How long have you lived here?" I enquired.

"Seventy-five years—I was born here."

"Was it before *that*?" I asked in a low voice.

Again he shook his head like a toy mandarin.

"Oh! then you *remember*?"

"Oh, massa. I only piccaninny," and without another word he hastily shuffled away.

I was about to pursue him, but I heard a call from George.

"Come on, Vernon, unless you want to live and die here; we're all waiting."

Thus summoned, I mounted my horse and, with all speed, followed the others down the avenue, but half way to the gate I turned and looked back, and the picture of that great, silent, forgotten home, is imprinted on my mind for ever.

Our headquarters were the delightful, well-appointed residence of George's cousins, the Middletons, and a house full of gay young faces presented an extraordinary contrast to our recent domicile. We were welcomed and made much of, especially by the ladies of the party, and treated like long-lost civilised castaways.

Of course, we were compelled to undergo an exhaustive cross-examination as to where we had been, and what we had been doing. George and Van Boom were spokesmen, and alternately related our experience. They told all about our discovery of the wonderful old mansion, which might have been dug up in Devonshire—and planted boldly among the Carolina rice fields!

As they described it, I noticed that the general interest waxed with every sentence, and at last Mr. Middleton exclaimed:

"You don't mean to say, you've all passed a night at Whitehall, and returned alive?"

"Very much alive," rejoined Van Boom, "in fact, if I hadn't spent the night there, I doubt if you'd ever have seen me again. I was completely done. What's the matter with the place?"

"I wish I could tell you," replied Miss Middleton, the daughter of the house. "Daddy" (this to her father), "you must know *something* about it—don't you rent part of the plantation?"

"Yes—that's a different thing to renting the house," he replied evasively, "the folk it belongs to have no use for it—they live in Venice."

"I don't wonder," exclaimed Van Boom, "there's not much life about their ancestral halls. Didn't they ever try to let it?"

"Well—yes—they did, but it was no snap anyway. The blacks make out, it's got plenty of tenants already. They are a superstitious pack, and possibly like to have the place to themselves. Heyward, the man who owns it, got an inkling of their tales, and sent word to the overseer that if ever anyone opened their lips about ghosts, they were to be turned off the plantation."

"Oh—then there *is* a story?" said George, "of course there's never smoke without fire."

"Let us have the tale, true or untrue," urged Van Boom.

"And so none of you saw anything?" said Mrs. Middleton, and her searching gaze wandered round our party.

"No," responded Van Boom, "we all slept soundly, and did ample justice to an ample breakfast—that's to say, all but Vernon. *You* looked rather chippy, old boy—you saw nothing? honour bright!"

"*Nothing*," I answered with absolute truth.

"Come then, father," pleaded Mrs. Middleton, "you may just tell us that story right away, you've always been fond of a mystery, and a sort of 'hush, hush' about that old house. Now these four gentlemen have stayed there, and seen nothing—I claim to hear the horror!"

Mr. Middleton deliberately sat down, crossed his legs, clasped his hands, and began in a sort of monotone: "Well, years and years ago, I believe, long before I came here, Whitehall belonged to a Mr. Heyward, a man of high English family; he was unmarried, and very eccentric."

"Of course, he was eccentric, if he was not married," put in Ellen Middleton.

"He would have nothing to do with his own relations in his later years, but shut himself up among his slaves, his books, and his gardens. He was reputed to be rich, and a bit of a miser. His health failed; I believe he was paralysed, and he was nursed and assiduously attended by a black boy called Sam, a slave who was greatly attached to him and in whom the old gentleman placed the most absolute confidence. Sam wrote his letters and managed his affairs to a certain extent; he waited on him, and sat up of a night, and, by all accounts, tended Mr. Heyward, as if he had been his own son.

"The story goes on, that one evening the two retired together as usual. Next morning, when the invalid's coffee was taken to him, his room was empty. He and Sam had both disappeared, and from that day to this, no trace of either the one or the other has ever been found. It was always believed that Mr. Heyward kept an immense sum of money in a certain bureau in his bedroom; but I understand that the contents of his bureau were a severe disappointment to his heirs!

"Naturally, there was an outcry and a strong suspicion of foul play, but whether Sam killed the old man, or the old man killed Sam, or someone else killed them both, was never discovered, and, as the mystery is now buried under the dust of sixty years, no one will never know the truth."

But—*I* knew.

La Carcassone

Two ladies stood gazing into a jeweller's shop in the Avenue de la Gare, Nice. Their attention was concentrated upon a case of rings which they were discussing with earnest gravity; it did not need the sound of "my dear", or "I assure you", to proclaim the fact that they were English—their costumes, hand-bags, fur neckties, were sufficient vouchers for their nationality.

The shorter and better-looking of the couple was Mrs. Wagstaffe, widow of an officer, a dark-eyed, voluble, vivacious little lady, who had seen a good deal of service—and the world—and was spending her fifth season on the Riviera. Her companion, Miss Tarr, was a tall, prim-looking person of about forty, who, by the recent death of an aged aunt, had become not merely emancipated, but an heiress—that is to say, she had eight hundred a year, and a loose thousand at her banker's. Released after twenty years of painful, domestic treadmill, she was her own mistress at last; her liberty was so recent, such a peculiar and unnatural condition, that at first Fanny Tarr did not know what to do with it, or herself. It seemed extraordinary not to be compelled to rise at seven (whether well or ill), not to have to dole out food and medicines, to read aloud for hours, to be pinched for money, and to render up an account of every spare moment, every spare stamp, to an exacting, selfish, and irascible tyrant. She had been guided to the Continent (a first visit) by her old schoolfellow, Letty Wagstaffe; they were staying at a well-known, fashionable hotel, and Miss Tarr was gradually beginning to realise that she might buy a new veil, a pair of gloves, or even a dress, without either fears or tears. She ventured to make acquaintances, receive and send letters, unread; she might devour novels, go to a theatre, wear a picture hat, or white kid gloves. All these forbidden pleasures were now hers, for poor Fanny knew as little of everyday gratifications as a child of six. Her aunt was a harsh, embittered old woman, who had imprisoned her youth without ruth; now the yoke was removed from Fanny's neck, and she was free to roam the world. At first like a creature long accustomed to confinement, she was reluctant to leave her cage, but her old friend had beckoned her and she had figuratively hopped forth! Behold her, staring into a well-known establishment, making up her mind to purchase her first ring!

Her relative, a rigid Puritan, had left no "gim-cracks, or gewgaws"—as she termed them—only a pair of hair bracelets, and a large black-and-gold memoriam brooch. Fanny Tarr was not exactly plain in appearance; she had a pale face, a set, demure expression, a fine head of hair, tightly tucked away, pretty eyebrows, and good teeth; if her nose was too large, and her eyes were too small for beauty her general appearance still possessed possibilities of which she was doubtless unaware. She had a craving to possess one or two pretty ornaments, but hitherto had not summoned up the courage necessary to expend a large sum on herself. Miss Tarr had been three delightful weeks in Nice, and had already mastered the words, "*oui*", "*merci*", "*entrez*", "*si'l vous plait*", and "*non*".

"Come, come, Fanny," exclaimed her friend, impatiently, "we cannot stand here all day! Do make up your mind! You've been to see these rings twenty times, and must know them by heart! What are you waiting for? It is your *own* money you are going to spend, and if you don't spend it on yourself, what are you saving it for? the cats' home?"

"You like the one with the black pearl best, don't you?" was Fanny's inconsequent reply.

"Yes—it is the one I would choose—such a beauty, a lovely pearl, set in fine brilliants. I call as a bargain for five hundred francs!"

"That is twenty pounds, is it not? I call it frightfully expensive. Well, of course, it is a big pearl, but I like the opal one, it has a sort of red spark in it, that shines like fire—"

"But opals are so unlucky. I can't bear them. They are malevolent stones."

"How can you talk such nonsense, Letty? You are an educated lady and a professing Christian! I feel quite *sorry* to hear you. Come; we will go in and look at the rings. No harm in that. But I really think a ring would be an extravagance—"

The case was brought out of the window, at Mrs. Wagstaffe's request, and Miss Tarr, having seated herself and removed her gloves, enjoyed the satisfaction of trying ring after ring upon her pretty and delicate fingers. After long demur, and many whisperings, the opal was her selection; it was a splendid stone, of fine size, set around in brilliants. She put it on several times, and each time she became more fascinated; it was surprisingly showy, and somehow seemed to dim the glories of the black pearl, the emerald, the turquoise, and the catseye.

"I like this one," she announced at last, "and I will take it. Twenty pounds, did you say?" she added, addressing the shopman, who luckily spoke English.

"Yes, and very cheap, a beautiful old ring, it is worth double."

"Then why—?" and she paused, and looked doubtful.

"Oh, well, madam, opals are out of fashion, also it is secondhand—a great *occasion!*"

"Secondhand!" she repeated, removing the ring as she spoke. In her narrow experience a secondhand article was improper.

"You see," he resumed, now leaning over, and speaking confidently, "we do a good deal of business with ladies who—gamble—at Monte Carlo. When they lose, they sell; when they win, they buy. Here, for instance," and he pulled out a drawer, "is a really beautiful neck ornament a customer brought yesterday, an emerald and diamond pendant. She will take ninety pounds; it is worth three times the money; you can see that for yourself!"

"Oh, how lovely!" exclaimed Mrs. Wagstaffe, "and how cheap!"

Miss Tarr one more slipped the opal ring on her finger, and held out her hand for the ornament. It bore the closest inspection, the workmanship was exquisite; she turned it about, held it towards the light, then against her dress, and glanced over at her reflection in the mirror.

"Did you ever see anything so pretty?" she said to her companion, who nodded a prompt assent.

Then, to her amazement, Fanny continued, "I mean to have it! I've nothing to wear on my neck of an evening."

"Oh, well, you cannot do better than that," said Mrs. Wagstaffe, with decision.

"Have you any more bargains?" inquired the customer of the shopman, "any brooches?"

"Yes, a diamond shell, a beautiful model," and he produced a pale blue velvet case. "It would go well with the pendant."

The brooch looked tempting as it sparkled on its velvet bed; the price was to correspond—only thirty pounds.

Fanny Tarr fingered it affectionately for some minutes, and then said, "Oh yes it *is* beautiful. I'll take it, too. Now, have you any pretty little watches with diamond settings?

I think"—turning to her astounded companion—"that I really ought to have a modern watch, instead of the old warming-pan that belonged to Aunt Susannah."

"Yes but why not wait a little, dear?"

"Why *wait*? You are the last person to ask that, Letty. Did you not almost drive me in here a quarter of an hour ago, and now I'm making up for lost time."

"You are, indeed!" asserted Mrs. Wagstaffe, as she saw her lately timid friend, boldly select a little jewelled watch, price forty guineas.

"A perfect darling!" according to its happy purchaser, who, in twenty minutes' time, had invested in jewellery to the extent of nearly two hundred pounds. Was this the same individual who had haggled over the price of a hair brush that same morning? She looked strangely different. No longer prim and demure, but impulsive, restless, animated; two bright spots brightened her usually pallid cheeks, and her small, dark eyes glittered with excitement.

She was actually requesting "to be shown some bracelets and chains", when Mrs. Wagstaffe rose, and said, "Really, Fanny, I will not allow you to buy the *whole* shop! You have laid out enough for one morning. Come along!"

Fanny, the meek and gentle, seemed inclined to remonstrate and rebel, but eventually agreed to defer further outlay. It was arranged that the articles were to be paid for by cheque on delivery, and, with a sigh of regret, Miss Tarr removed the opal ring from her finger and handed it over the counter, when it was presently shut up in its own little velvet case.

Then the two ladies bowed themselves out of the establishment, and departed towards Cimiez.

"What a howler you've gone! Fanny, my dear," exclaimed her friend, "you began with wishing for a little turquoise ring at one hundred francs, and you have spent two hundred pounds. I suppose, in buying jewellery, *l'appétit vient en mangeant*. But it is so unlike you. I fail to understand it!"

"Neither can I," burst out Miss Tarr, who turned to her with a frightened face. "I cannot imagine *what* possessed me! Something seemed to get into my head, and say, 'Buy! buy! buy! you must have these things; it is no matter about money!' "

"Well, I've heard of wine, but never of jewels, going to a person's head. Still, I am glad you bought them in a moment of courage. Now you can have them always, and they will be a pleasure to you for life; and you really ought to have some ornaments, a woman in your position!"

"But two hundred pounds!" wailed Fanny. "Two hundred pounds would have given me the education which Aunt Susannah grudged. Just think of spending two hundred pounds in twenty minutes! I declare I feel quite *sick*! I've only eleven hundred lying at Coutts."

"Besides your income—it's a sum apart!"

"Yes, a sort of pocket money."

"Well I'd be inclined to spend every penny on myself—on things that you ought to have enjoyed years ago."

"What things? What sort of things?"

"Prom dresses, travelling, sight seeing, lessons, charities, books, souvenirs, jewels—You have the jewels."

The purchases were delivered that same afternoon, and at once transformed the sallow and remorseful Fanny, into a smiling, self-confident, and complacent lady. At dinner she actually wore them all: brooch, pendant, watch, and ring.

They seemed to give her assurance and self-reliance—the hitherto timid, silent spinster—who had preferred to forego salt sooner than ask it of a stranger—took part in general conversation, advanced her opinions, and laid down the law.

What had come to her friend? Mrs. Wagstaffe looked on in helpless bewilderment. Was it a mental case?

Hitherto, Fan had never said boo to a goose; now she was cackling louder than any goose in the company, and people listened attentively. Especially Colonel Harker, an elderly bachelor who roamed the Continent—Riviera in winter, Switzerland in summer. He had never believed that Miss Tarr had money till now; hitherto she resembled a half-starved, poor relation, but here she was, decorated with diamonds, and looking most expensive. How she had come out of her shell! She was positively becoming festive, and ordering champagne, she who, hitherto, had been a strict teetotaller! Well, women were strange!

The morning after her shopping, as Miss Tarr did not appear, her friend went to seek her, and was astonished to find the usually early bird still in her nest. The hour, eleven o'clock!

"Yes," she cried, "it's too great a fag getting up. There's nothing to do till the afternoon, you know. It's so nice lying here, and reading a jolly novel!"

"You call this a jolly novel?" exclaimed Mrs. Wagstaffe, as she picked at a book of too notorious fame. "Why, I thought you never touched such grubby things, or, indeed, any novels at all."

"Oh, it's never too late to mend!" was the amazing rejoinder. "I'm awfully pleased with my purchases," here she held up her hand and exhibited the ring; "they made quite a little sensation last night. If a woman has no fascinations, I can recommend jewellery; it attracts both sexes."

"Oh yes; but it is only a passing glance. Why, I declare you have put wavers in your hair!"

"Yes, but I am going today to get a lesson in hairdressing. I asked Miss Vapton, and she recommends me to go to Refraicheur, and I will spend the afternoon in learning a new style of *coiffure*. You won't know me, dear. Now run away, I must get up!"

Miss Tarr's words were prophetic. Her companion lost sight of her for several hours after *déjeuner*. She was not to be found in the hotel. No one had seen her, and Mrs. Wagstaffe, who began to feel seriously uneasy, was about to ascend to her room to dress for dinner, when an apparently strange lady swept into the lift. A lady in a smart feather boa and a large blue hat, which covered a head of wonderfully dressed dark red hair!

"Letty," screamed the stranger, "is it possible that you don't know me?"

The liftman grinned, and Mrs. Wagstaffe, who was thunderstruck, rejoined, "Why should I not know you, Fanny?"

"Oh, half-a-dozen 'whys'," she retorted audaciously. "Come along to my room. I've so much to tell you."

"I am awaiting information," said Mrs. Wagstaffe, as she took a seat in her transformed companion's third-floor bedroom "But, do tell me; why have you dyed your hair?"

"Renovated," she corrected, tossing off her large hat. "I've such crowds of hair. The process took four solid hours, and cost—but it is well worth it. Don't I look fashionable, with all this big puff round my face?" And she gazed at herself with rapture.

"But what possessed you?" asked her friend, examining her with discriminating and censorious eyes.

"The desire to be smart, admired, and in the swim!"

"*Fanny!*" she expostulated.

"Why not, pray?" she demanded, hands on hips, "better late than never, that is my motto, and a phoenix is my crest! I've little enough time to enjoy myself. I mean now, to make time and money *fly*."

"What have you been buying?"

"Just this hat—my hair would not *fit* the other—this boa, eight pounds—a dozen pairs of white gloves, and some veils. I'm thirty-eight, but my hair and figure are young! With a little dressing up, I'll do!"

Mrs. Wagstaffe suddenly realised that she was listening to personality, and there was a piercing, not to say bold, expression in Fanny's eyes, utterly alien to her former meek character. At last she stammered, "But—but how can you dare to come down so utterly metamorphosed? Your hair brown and grey at *déjeuner*, dark red at dinner—it is too sudden."

"A sudden dying! I do not intend to go to table at all. I shall dine in the restaurant. You dine too, and we'll have a bottle of champagne. If anyone inquiries, you may tell them that a *shock* has turned my hair red. I do think it's lovely!"

To which Mrs. Wagstaffe retorted, "I will tell them your head is turned."

"So it is, but why? I feel myself utterly different, quite daring and bold and reckless, ready to dance, go to the theatre—or even to the gambling!"

"If you have decided to have this hair always, I think we must really leave the hotel."

"Yes, it will stand as it is for three weeks. The man guaranteed that, on his honour as a *teinturier*. I think the move a good idea. I'll not show, but let us move to Monte Carlo tomorrow. Wire for rooms at the 'Paris'."

"But, my dear Fanny, it is so expensive. I never could afford it," expostulated Mrs. Wagstaffe.

"Oh, bother expense! I'll pay for both. Yes, I really mean it. A short life and a merry one! When old 'stick-in-the-mud', my solicitor at home, sees my cheques, won't he stare! I intend to have a good time, and that I tell you. What do *you* say?"

"But you ought to go to bed, have ice on your head, and see a doctor. I'm sure you are over-wrought and hysterical."

"Nonsense! We'll go down and have our champagne iced, and then, perhaps, we will see *two* doctors!"

Mrs. Wagstaffe lay awake till dawn, wondering what had caused such a sudden and complete revolution in the character of Fanny Tarr—water drinker, Puritan, and prude!

In a week's time Mrs. Wagstaffe and her gay friend were well known by sight at Monte Carlo. Fanny, arrayed in the latest mode, the most expensive and remarkable hats and gowns, really presented a striking and attractive figure, and, being thin to emaciation, she carried off the frills and flounces of the period with triumphant elegance.

The first time she had seen the gambling-rooms she spoke of them with bated breath as "the mouth of hell". This was shortly after her arrival at Nice. Now she frequented them, and daily spent hours at the tables.

It was marvellous how soon she learned the rules of *"trente et quarante"* and *"rouge et noir"*, how soon she began to chatter of "douzaines" and *"transversals"*, and "runs on the red", and, whatever soul she had, was surrendered to play.

She invariably sat at one table, in one place, with her card and her pile of money before her, her pencil in her ungloved hand, Miss Tarr was a wild and feverish gambler, and won at first amply sufficient to embolden her, and dazzle her poor brain.

When not at the rooms, or the theatre, she chattered incessantly of the tables, how this man had won ten thousand francs, and that one had lost and disappeared. As she was gay, talkative, smartly dressed, and hospitable, she picked up a good many friends, among these Colonel Harker (who, at inconvenient expense, had followed her from Nice, and taken up his quarters at the "Paris")—nor was he the only man who would have been glad to marry the jaunty, open-handed Miss Tarr. It was told that her hair was "fashionable", her toilettes a vivid scarlet, bright blue, or apple-green, and her laugh loud, but she was a bold, successful gambler, and so good-natured! Lunches at Ciros, motor trips to San Remo, dinners at the "Paris", and, although her appearance was *risqué* and remarkable, her conversation and morals, were models of propriety.

One day a wizened old gentleman came and established himself beside her at the tables. He was French, and gambled on a system, with a roll of notes, a card, and a little silver image set before him, apparently for luck. He played irregularly, and when not occupied with his own game, took a certain amount of interest in Fanny Tarr's fortunes.

She was winning, and cleared off on one coup two thousand francs. As he had been losing, she glanced at him, and drew in her breath with a little gasp of exultation.

"Ah, I congratulate madam," he grunted, "especially as she sits in La Carcassonne's seat, and wears La Carcassonne's ring."

Fanny stared at her interrogator, and he continued: "She was very gay, and rich, and a fortunate gambler; she always sat in your chair. One day she had the misfortune to find that ring; she picked it up on the shore; they say it had a bad history. Anyway, it brought her ill luck. She lost everything; she even lost it. She gambled away all she possessed."

"And then what happened?" demanded Fanny in a breathless voice.

"Ah, madam, only the sea could tell you! Madam is happy and wins; may such good fortune continue, but—" and he paused significantly.

Fanny turned over her hand, and gazed at the ring of ill luck

"What do they say of it? Tell me!"

"They say—of course, it is mad folly—that it is ancient, one can see that—old as a poison ring—that each one who wears it, leaves with it the impress of a personality, and transfers her character to whoever owns it *next*. Those who possess it are never themselves. They represent the spirit of the former owner. You, madam, would therefore be La Carcassonne, but, of course, all this I say to you, is a foolish story. It was a jeweller who told me. Often they are liars, those jewellers." Then he suddenly pushed back his chair, and went away.

It was an astonishing but unpleasant fact that, soon after this conversation, Miss Fanny began to enter on a cycle of bad luck. It encompassed her day after day. Her ill fortune became as proverbial, as her good fortune had been. She tried every expedient; she played only in the morning, or only after dinner; she changed her table; she bought charms; she staked high, and let her stakes double. No; it was of no use! Then she became desperate—deaf to her friend's frantic remonstrances. Mrs. Wagstaffe, ashamed and alarmed, did all in her power to persuade Fanny to cease playing, and to return home, for, besides all her winnings, she had lost three thousand pounds, and gained a taste for gambling, rouge, cigarette-smoking, and champagne.

The little widow could not desert her friend—who was generously paying all her expenses. Formerly she was somewhat close fisted, and rarely made presents. Now the instant Mrs. Wagstaffe admired a hat, a fan, a parasol, Fanny would say, "You shall have it!" This is an attractive quality, and Fanny was most lavishly generous. But she was rowdy at times, she chaffed men, and sat with her elbows on the table, her legs crossed, and altogether adopted bold and ungraceful attitudes. She drank liqueurs, champagne and *café noir*, smoked dozens of cigarettes, lay in bed till the tables were open, and wore scarlet silk stockings, and quantities of jewellery. As for the opal ring, it was never removed from her finger.

In six short weeks, she was totally unrecognisable. Fanny Tarr, of Tranmere, Birkenhead, had disappeared, and given place to a woman with a loud voice, bad manners, the dress and air of a French actress, inclined to be bold, profuse, and dissipated.

One day, suddenly resolved to be either rich or ruined, Fanny went to the bank, wired to London, drew out almost all her available capital, and, with a stiff roll of notes in her hand-bag, repaired to the rooms. There she hovered around in search of 'luck', and luck on this occasion seemed to have settled itself at the suicides' table—the first on the left in the middle room. At this she halted, and at the first opportunity seized upon a chair. Something, a giddiness, seemed to have got into her head—the fever, the madness, the intoxication of gambling—and, regardless of the fact that she was staking her fortune and future, she put down the maximum again and again, and lost, and lost, and lost. When she had come to her last twenty-franc piece, she rose, flung away her empty bag, and walked forth, looking as desperate and distracted as some others who had left the same portal. To think, that in two hours' time she had squandered five thousand pounds! She called a little carriage, and drove out to Monaco, climbed up the gardens there, sat down over the sea, and endeavoured to think. Two months ago she was a rich woman (for her); now, after eight weeks of feverish excitement, dissipation, and extravagance, she was again poor. She had about two hundred a year, and her clothes, jewels—yes, and her debts—dress-makers' and hotel bills.

How could she go back to her old life? Impossible! better be dead. Yes; she would do like La Carcassonne—jump over the cliff, and end it all.

Dying was so much easier than living. The jewellery—well, it would be a pity to waste it on the sea. She would tie it up in her handkerchief, and leave it with a note for poor Letty. With this intention, she sat down, pencilled a few lines on a leaf of her notebook, then proceeded to remove watch, brooch, chain, bangles, and rings; last, not least, the opal.

As they lay together in a glittering heap in her lap, and she was preparing to tie them up in her handkerchief, her friend unexpectedly appeared round the corner. Was this telepathy or coincidence?

"Fanny," she exclaimed, "what *are* you doing here all alone?"

"I've come for a walk," she answered shortly.

"But why have you got all your chains and rings in your lap?" (Certainly her mind was unhinged!)

"I wanted to get rid of them—and of myself. Letty, as I sit here, I feel so odd—as if I'd come back out of a long illness." And she suddenly removed her hat, and stared at her friend with a perfectly sane pair of eyes— the usually dull eyes of Fanny Tarr.

"I've been gambling. Something possessed me, forced me along, and drove me to do it. I cannot think why! and I've lost all my fortune, except about two hundred a year, and I've been *mad*! Now I feel sane; nothing would ever take me into that horrible place again."

"Where you have lost thousands! Oh, Fanny! What made you do it?"

"Perhaps this ring," holding it in the hollow of the hand, where it seemed to burn like a hot spark, or the fiery eye of an angry animal.

"Ring?" repeated Mrs. Wagstaffe, "why, I thought you were so fond of it; you never took it off, day or night."

"Yes, I've felt odd ever since I bought it, and I've behaved strangely, have I not? Not like *myself*?"

Mrs. Wagstaffe nodded an emphatic assent.

"No wonder; for all the time, if the old man spoke the truth, I have been a Frenchwoman—an actress, called La Carcassonne. She owned the ring; she killed herself, when she was ruined, and the idea is, that the last wearer of the ring projects her spirit into the next owner. It is not pleasant, but I think it is *true*, and that I, for the last two months, have been possessed by the individuality of a French dancer. Now," rising suddenly, and approaching the parapet, "Venice wedded the Adriatic with a ring. I," and she flung the opal high into the air, "offer this *wicked* ring to the Mediterranean."

"Oh, Fanny, you've wasted twenty pounds!" screamed her friend.

"But I've got rid of La Carcassonne! In future I'm going to be—I am—myself. I am sorry for my lunacy, but you must help me to save the remainder of my little fortune, sell the jewellery, pay bills, and clear out for home."

"As soon as you like. The sooner the better," agreed Mrs. Wagstaffe.

"Today, tonight if possible!" said Fanny, now standing up, and tossing the handkerchief and contents to her friend. "Try and sell these. I'm afraid of them," and the face she turned on her listener was white, scared, and haggard. "I've been *possessed*! To think of it!" And she shuddered.

"Nonsense, Fanny; you've been a little off your head; it was a fit of temporary insanity, the result of unaccustomed liberty, temptation, and spirits."

"Spirits! Yes, it was the opal ring, and the spirit of La Carcassonne. Nothing, nothing will ever persuade me otherwise. It was an accursed ring; it compelled me to wear it always. Well, now it is gone, and she is gone, I am myself again, am I not?" She paused and gazed at her friend with a pair of solemn little anxious eyes.

"I hope so, most sincerely, my dear."

"You have been so good to me, Letty. I shall never forget it. What a life I have led you—or, rather, what a life *she* has led us both!"

"Come now, Fanny, be really your own sensible self, and don't talk folly. Let us go home at once, and pack, and pay bills, and get away from all this!"

"Yes; and I've got away from her. Do you know, as I stood leaning over this parapet half-an-hour ago, and thinking of my losses and miseries, something seemed to whisper to me: '*Jump*! It will all be over in a few seconds.' I know it was that devilish opal. Oh yes, I'm coming; and for the future I intend to be thoroughly commonplace and sensible. And after all, Letty, it was *you* who tempted me into the jeweller's shop in Nice. Only for you, I would never have bought that diabolical ring, and fallen under the influence of its former owner—a dissipated, painted Jezebel!"

Mrs. Ponsonby's Dream

*"I would not spend another such a night
Though 'twere to bring a world of happy days."*

– Richard III.

One winter's day sixty years ago, when the climate of Ireland, in spite of what aged people declare to the contrary, was quite as moist as it is now, a tall, erect, dark woman stood watching the rain stream down the windows of a front drawing-room in Mountjoy Square. She wore her hair in bands, and was dressed in a puce tabinet gown, with a low neck, and very tight long sleeves—in fact, the fashion of both coiffure and sleeves would be deemed *à la mode* at present—and her expression of sullen discontent with the weather is, in these latitudes, never out of date.

As she yawned and drummed upon the panes with a much beringed hand, the door opened, and another lady, older and plainer than herself, wearing a massive beaver bonnet, a damp pelisse, and carrying a heavy morocco box, hurried into the room.

"It's turned out shockingly wet," she exclaimed, "so I took a hackney coach from the Bank. I fetched your diamonds, you see, and I've ordered the brown posters for the Britzka tomorrow."

"And I was hoping that you could not get them," said her sister peevishly, turning round as she spoke.

"La, Sally, what freak have you got now?"—setting down the jewel-case, and staring with eyes of dismay.

"It's no freak, my good Nancy, but a dream—a warning, and I never felt so ill-disposed to spend a week at Williamsfort since I was born."

"Gracious patience, Sal! but Richard will be sorely put out if you fail him."

"I suppose he will," glancing at an open letter in her hand, which was a great cumbersome affair, the size of a pocket-handkerchief, bearing a red seal and a nobleman's frank. It was not from her lover, but from her only brother—a wealthy bachelor—and said:

Dear Sal

The Emersons, Hamiltons, and Moores, and six men are coming on Tuesday for the Assizes and ball. I should expect you, as usual, to play hostess. Order post-horses in time, and I'll send a pair to meet you at the thirteenth milestone. Don't be later than three o'clock—we dine at four.

Your affectionate brother,

R. Connor.

P.S.—Pray bring the oysters from Jury's and oblige.

"Nancy," said her sister, suddenly sitting down, "tell me honestly do you believe in dreams?"

"In dreams—no—but I must confess that I think there is something in cup-tossing."

"Pooh—that is rare folly! Pray, did you never have a dream that haunted you, and terrified you, and made you ill at ease?"

"Nay, I'm a sound sleeper, and the worst thing I ever dreamt was, that I was married," and she wheezed and giggled ridiculously.

"And that means a death," remarked Mrs. Ponsonby. "Well, I had an awful experience last night, and you know how poorly I was today, and thought not to rise. I believe I have received a warning not to go to Williamsfort," solemnly nodding her head,

"La, my dear sister Sally, what talk is this for a sensible creature like yourself! I do protest you are joking."

"At least, you shall listen and judge, my good Nancy. I dreamt that I drove up to the house a little late. The door was opened by a strange young man, with a dark sinister face, I immediately asked for old John, and he replied that he was dead—had died very suddenly—whereupon I felt mightily shocked and upset. But I noticed that all the time this wretch was speaking to me, and assisting me to alight, his eyes were resolutely fastened on the jewelled clasps of my furred travelling pelisse. At last Richard appeared in a vast flurry, and confirmed the ill news of poor John's death—assured me that the company were all assembled, and hurried me off to dress. I wore my crimson velvet, all my diamonds, and even my stomacher, to do dear Dick honour, and went downstairs, still sorely discomposed, though I had frequent recourse to my smelling-salts. At dinner—which was, as usual, well cooked and served—I was always catching the new butler's gaze whenever I looked up; his attention appeared to be riveted on me—and my jewels. After the gentleman had joined us, which was not until late, we played cards, and I lost nigh twenty-three guineas at Faro to my Lady Susan. It's my belief she cheats—see how real was my dream."

Miss Nancy nodded her head, but made no remark.

"We retired late. I lay in the lattice chamber, which, you know, has a separate passage, and a dressing-room opening into both room and passage. Well, I locked one door, but not the one communicating with the dressing-closet—and presently went to bed. I was just dozing off when I heard soft, stealthy steps in the passage. The handle turned but the door was fast. In a few seconds the dressing-room was entered very cautiously, and then the door into my room. Through my eyelashes I watched the new butler creep in, and by the firelight I saw him approach the bed on tip-toe, a long knife in his hand; and then, thank Heaven, I awoke! My heart was beating so terribly fast that I never closed an eye the whole night, and more than once I felt about to swoon."

"It certainly sounds as real as a true tale," said her sister slowly "But it was only the potted boar's head you had for supper!" she added soothingly.

"It was a solemn warning, I'll swear; and I'm in more than half a mind to send an excuse to Dick, and say I have a bad attack of the vapours."

"Do not, sister Sally; if you disoblige Richard for a mere dream, he will be mortally incensed. He likes to see you at the head of the table: your celebrated jewels make a rare show; and you are still a very personable and agreeable woman. I tell you that if old John has gone, we would have had tidings of his death. Of course, there is no new butler; and really, sister, you amaze me—you are generally so brave! That time the mail-coach upset in the snowdrift, you never minded one bit, whilst I was screaming like a Gib cat."

Mrs. Ponsonby had not another word to say; she was sensible of derision in her sister's looks; Nancy's sound com- monsense carried the day, and so restored her confidence and dispelled her presentiments, that the next afternoon saw the widow depart in her own carriage, along with her best gowns, her diamonds, and her maid.

It was nearly four o'clock when a pair of smoking horses trotted up the long winding avenue to Williamsfort. Mrs. Ponsonby, having constantly consulted her watch, was in a fever of nervousness, for her brother was punctuality itself, and would be seriously put out by her tardy arrival. The door was opened; she gave a little stifled cry—for the dark man of her dream stood on the threshold! She felt inclined to shriek, but after a pause faintly inquired for "old John—where is he?"

"He is dead, your ladyship; he was taken suddenly five days ago," was the glib reply, "and buried on Monday—"

Mr. Connor now appeared, and formally conducted his sister into the house, but she felt so weak that she could scarcely crawl into a sitting room, and when she had found a seat, burst into tears, and piteously demanded another pair of horses, and permission to return to town within half an hour.

Her brother instantly administered his panacea for all ills, from nerves to toothache—a glass of old port; and as the lady recovered her voice and her composure, listened to her story in crimson amazement.

" 'Tis true that old John died very suddenly—of gout to the stomach; but this new fellow has excellent testimonials. However, lock all your doors tonight, Sal, and when you hear a sound, ring your bell—we will keep guard—and you will be as safe as if you were in a church. Now hurry and dress, my good Sally; the company are waiting, and the Judge, I know, is hungry, and so am I."

Everything fell out precisely as in Mrs. Ponsonby's dream. She occupied the isolated lattice chamber. She noticed the butler's persistent contemplation of her diamonds. She lost heavily at Faro—and Lady Susan won. Pale enough after her journey and money losses, the hostess at last retired, and having dismissed her maid—who complained of the megrims, and flatly declined to sleep in the dressing-room—locked all doors, and went to bed.

About one o'clock, as she lay wide awake, her expectant ear caught stealthy footsteps, then a handle turned. She sprang out on the floor, tore at her bell, and then fainted. Meanwhile, Mr. Connor and his friends rushed headlong towards her room, and discovered, half concealed in a dark corner in the passage, the new butler, in his stockinged feet, carrying a basket of wood.

"What"—string of fashionable oaths—"are you doing up here?" demanded his master, taking him roughly by the collar.

"The servant-maids were tired, and asked me to carry up firing to the rooms," was the ready reply.

"Firing! At one in the morning?" giving the basket an angry kick. Out fell the wood, and out fell a long glittering knife—which spoke for itself.

The younger men now hurried the culprit downstairs, and locked him securely in his own apartment intending to deliver him over the next morning into the arms of the law.

But when they went to open the door and hand the new butler (and old burglar) to the police, it was discovered that the bird had flown! A sheet fluttering from the window was all that remained of the realisation of Mrs. Ponsonby's Dream.

The Door Ajar

Two years ago, when my youngest brother, an artist, was ordered abroad, I was the sister selected to accompany him to the south of France. Here, by mutual consent, we avoided fashionable resorts and palatial hotels, partly from motives of economy, partly choice, and were so fortunate as to discover a delightful little spot, with a climate to correspond, in a nook at the foot of the Pyrenees. Our hotel was comfortable, unpretentious, and moderate. In the river which flowed beneath our windows was excellent trout-fishing; the neighbourhood was lovely, and Hubert found a bewildering number of subjects for his sketch-book—exquisite bits of water, mountains, foliage, ancient Basque houses, and dignified monastic buildings.

Between fishing, sketching, and exploring we spent most of the time out of doors. Within, our fellow-guests were a pleasant, sociable company, chiefly English. Among them was Professor Baines, a learned and celebrated individual, with a fine head, a benevolent expression, and a beard reaching half way down his waistcoat. He had sought this sunny, secluded spot solely for a "rest cure", and in order to evade notoriety and the daily post. I often watched him pacing a long, grassy, tree-shaded path overlooking the river, his chin on his breast his hands locked behind him, his mind doubtless among the stars. There were also Mrs. Wynne, a tall, fair young woman, whose husband was in India, and her curly-headed son Bobby, brimming over with high spirits and energy; his merry chatter and his rapid, springing footsteps resounded through the stairs and passages, and kept us all alive. Although an only child, he was not in the least spoilt, but a fine, manly, good-hearted little fellow, just a trifle hampered by an exuberant vitality, and the newly-acquired *joie de vivre*. Finally, Colonel and Mrs. Lille, an Anglo-Indian couple, friends of Mrs. Wynne. The lady was elegant, faded, somewhat of a *malade imaginaire*, devoted to dress, and to a tiny dog not much bigger than a rat. Her husband was a wiry, bronzed warrior, with an immense white moustache, a pleasant, cordial manner, a fund of reminiscence, and an energy scarcely surpassed by that of Bobby Wynne. The two were playmates and close friends.

Occasionally we combined (all but Mrs. Lille) and made a party to visit some old village or monastery in the neighbourhood, and in order fitly to celebrate Bobby's seventh birthday we arranged an expedition to a venerable town near the Spanish frontier. This was an expedition of a more ambitious type, for we travelled by rail, journeying along in a lazy fashion by the river, in and out among the mountains, winding higher and still higher with every leisurely mile. At last we reached a narrow valley, at the far end of which was our destination. Here the train, to Bobby's amazement, came to a full stop. He could not understand *why* it went no farther; he seemed to think it should always "go on", and plied us with maddening questions. The truth was, we were now in a *cul-de-sac*, surrounded on three sides by mountains; and, for my own part, I was surprised that a railway should be here at all!

Vidarry consisted or but one long, straggling street, lined with tile-roofed Spanish houses. Half way up this town stood an ancient Basque church; its encompassing cemetery seemed to be one mass of iris; the crosses and tombstones emerged, so to speak, from a very sea of purple; the old walls of the edifice were draped in exquisite mauve wisteria, and this colouring, combined with its red roof, presented a brilliant picture. Parallel with the town ran a river, and on a hill across the water was an imposing and turreted grey château, outlined in sharp relief, and, as it were, framed by a background of deep blue mountains Having exhausted the sights of Vidarry—the church, the one shop, the arrival of a ramshackle diligence drawn by three mules—we made our way to the inn, which proved to be equally old-fashioned and clean. Here, in a sitting room commanding a view of bridge and château, we speedily disposed of coffee, bread and butter, preserves and cake. Then we examined the apartment, and discovered photographs of Madame's relations (Madame was a brisk, dark-eyed, charming little Basque). There were a few tawdry vases, some old calendars, a venerable copy of *Le Petite Gironde*—that was all. Our train was not due to start for two mortal hours. We had bungled the local "Bradshaw". What could we do to kill time? Madame kindly exhibited her best bedroom, her vegetable garden, her rabbits; and yet we were not happy.

"Tiens!" she exclaimed suddenly, "I have it; there is the Château. The family are in Paris, but a friend of mine, *une fermière*, has the keys. She will do much for me. I will send."

"Yes; by all means," urged Mrs. Wynne, who spoke fluent French. "I do enjoy seeing old places."

"But what is there to see?" inquired Hubert, in a grumbling voice. He was rather querulous, for it had been a long and disappointing day.

"It is very old, and there are beautiful gardens and parterres, and, inside, pictures—*magnifique, splendide*," raising her little plump hands.

"Oh!" more eagerly, "pictures! What sort?"

"Wonderful, people say. Above all, one worth, oh—this room full of money."

"Whom is it by?"

"Ah! that no one knows; some say a saint painted it."

"And who is the owner of the Château?"

"Madame de la Vaye; she lives in Paris—here it is so *triste*. Once they were great folk, and had riches and honours; now all that remains to her is the Château and the pictures."

"If they are hard up, I wonder they don't sell the pictures," put in Colonel Lille, in most atrocious French; then aside to us. "It is what *we* did."

"Pardon, monsieur, but there is some family deed; the pictures must never leave the Château de la Vaye, or certainly they would have gone many years ago. Ah! here comes *le petit* with the keys. It is well; Madame Colbert will oblige."

We had soon trooped across a narrow old one-arched bridge and along a path which ran between the river and a high wall enclosing the demesne of the Château, entered a gate, and found ourselves in a pretty park. The month was April, the lilac was out, the camellias too; magnolias were budding, and the lower part of the great house was, like the chapel, covered with wisteria. Without, all was so fair to see; it seemed a pity that it was so forlorn and deserted. The interior was oppressively gloomy, until the bustling caretaker flung open the shutters, and proudly displayed the grand saloon, the staircase, the long gallery, all lined with pictures—portraits or Scriptural subjects, and most entirely of the Spanish school. Hubert hummed and hawed, and criticised and sneered; but he admitted that there were two Murillos and at least one Velasquez, worth, as our hostess had said, a great price.

Little Bobby, who was in the wildest spirits, had at first declared against coming into the funny old ugly house. He desired to remain outside and chase butterflies; but his mother, knowing his volatile character, would not trust him out of her sight, and drove him indoors, a light-hearted, skipping figure, with a sailor hat on the back of his sunny curls. As he began to caper about the echoing rooms, which were really most interesting, I noticed that he had gradually become curiously quiet and silent. The gloomy old Château seemed to have cast a spell upon the child. I watched him as he went and stood for a long time gazing out of a window which overlooked the town and river, and when at last he turned his face towards me it had a strange, haggard, almost scared expression.

At the far end of the gallery, Madame Colbert drew our attention to a half-length picture of a knight in armour; it was called "Saint George", and was an undoubtedly admirable painting. There was much character in the bold, distinguished, absorbing face; the eyes seemed to shine out of the canvas, and to hold the spectator in a manner curiously lifelike.

"*Voilà!* It is worth a fortune," boasted Madame Colbert. "People come from far to look at this alone—and yet no one can say who painted it."

"Yes," muttered the Professor, "like that wonderful wooden figure of the Virgin at Nuremburg—the inspired artist is unknown."

Little Bobby, who had pushed his way among us, and stood riveted before the portrait, seemed fascinated, and unable to take his eyes from the face.

"You like it, sonny, don't you?" said his mother. "It is the portrait of a great soldier. No one can tell who painted it, but that does not matter; it is beautiful, is it not?"

"Yes," he assented gravely; then, after a moment's silence, he added the startling announcement—"*I* know who painted it."

"What?"

"Yes. I did every single bit of it *myself*."

"Oh, my dear silly child," expostulated Mrs. Wynne, "how can you talk such utter nonsense?"

"It is not nonsense," he rejoined, with blazing eyes, and giving his little foot a stamp; "it is true—true—true. Do I ever tell lies?" His eyes were dilated, and his round, rosy face seemed suddenly to have become thin and wan.

"But, dearest boy, you have only seen it for the first time five minutes ago, and you know you cannot even draw a straight line. Such talk is not at all funny."

"But it is true, true," he stammered, and his eyes were full of tears. "I did paint that in a big cold room—the floor was of stone"; here he shivered visibly. "Yes, I can remember it all right." And he gazed up at his mother with tragic face.

Mrs. Wynne returned his look with an expression of pained amazement, not unmingled with anxiety. Was the child's brain altered? She went up to him, removed his straw hat, and ran her hand through his curls.

"Have you a headache, darling?"

"No," and he pushed her away, half crying. "You think I am a story-teller, and won't believe me." And his lip trembled.

"What is it all about, my little man?" said the Professor. "Why won't they believe you?"

"Because," raising his voice almost to a shout, "I said I painted that—and I *did*." Here he pointed to the picture with his small, childish hand—a hand not large enough to wield a brush.

"You did," assented the Professor, "but when?"

"Oh, how can I tell you?"—impatiently. "It's all ever so long ago; I forget. I cannot see anything but the picture, and the river. One day—a man was drowned by the bridge; his name was Roco—I remember that—and—if you will look at the picture at the back, I know there are three red crosses on the canvas—my mark—yes, *my* mark."

"I'm afraid the poor child has had a touch of the sun," said his mother, turning to us. "He *will* run about without his hat." Then to him, "Very well, darling, of course; don't

I always believe you? Now come away with me into the pretty garden, and we will get out of this gloomy castle as fast as we can. I don't like it."

Without the smallest reluctance, or another glance at the picture, the child put his hand in hers, and obediently trotted off down the gallery.

"Strange!" exclaimed the Professor. "One never *quite* knows—what a child forgets—or remembers! I must confess I'd like to have the picture turned about—I suppose it can be done?" and he nodded to me, put his hand in his pocket, and produced a ten-franc piece.

In a remote place like Vidarry a ten-franc piece can do great things. With but little trouble, and a considerable amount of talk, and dusting, the celebrated picture of "St. George" was removed from the wall, and there, indeed, on the back of the canvas, were three large blurred crosses in faded red paint!

"You and I understand it, Colonel," said the Professor. "We have been in the East, where people believe, as an everyday fact, in reincarnation."

The Colonel nodded emphatically, and added, "Yes, but here—"

"Here the child has had a glimpse, a flash, of one of his former lives. He will forget it, it will never return."

"Surely you don't think there's anything in it?" protested Hubert. "Reincarnation is rubbish."

The Professor merely smiled, he and the Colonel looked at one another significantly, and the Professor replied; "I believe in the evolution of the body, and the evolution of the soul. There! I think I hear Mrs. Wynne calling," and he hurried towards the stairs.

Out in front of the Château we found Mrs. Wynne, declaiming with both arms and a parasol, "We shall be late for the train; we have only ten minutes."

Meanwhile Bobby, hat in hand, was chasing butterflies; yes, already the door was closed, and Bobby was himself again.

"I say, what a time you have been looking at those ugly old pictures!" he cried, running up to the Colonel. "Just look at my beautiful orange butterfly! I shall have to keep him in my pocket till we get home to the chloroform bottle."

"Will you do a kind thing, my little man?" said the Professor "You have had a nice birthday—eh, haven't you?"

"Oh, jolly."

"Then let the poor butterfly go. His life means much to him, and so little to you."

"But it's such a beauty! Well"—and the child gazed gravely up at the Professor—"here goes," and, a second later, an orange-winged captive had fluttered away.

Little Bobby skipped and chattered in front of us all down the hill, and over the bridge to the station, where we found we had barely three minutes to spare. Once more we packed ourselves comfortably into a first class carriage, and were soon creeping away along the valley, and leaving Vidarry behind us. But I kept my gaze steadily fixed on the most prominent object in the landscape, until it was lost to sight.

What a curious scene had taken place in the gallery of that venerable prey Château! and the principal actor had already forgotten the part he had played. A cautious question elicited the reply, "Oh, I didn't like those bothering old pictures. I hate ugly black men." Evidently every trace of the "St. George" was erased from the child's memory, he was tired and drowsy, and presently fell sound asleep, with his fair head resting against his mother's shoulder. They made a pretty picture.

On the journey homeward, during a low voiced but animated discussion, I overheard the Professor mutter to his neighbour the Colonel:

"Oh yes, it was ajar for a few moments—a most rare occurrence—but now the door is closed for ever."

Mrs. Croker

Helen C. Black

The scene is a lovely view of the Wicklow Mountains, which seem as if divided into groups separated by precipitous ravines, generally straight and narrow. The declivities slope gently downwards in many places, terminating in glens and valleys. The lofty promontory of Bray Head rises to the height of some 800 feet above the level of the sea and, overhanging it, makes a conspicuous sea-mark. The landscape is wild and picturesque. Facing all this grandeur of nature by the south there stands, in about five acres of garden, lawn, and pleasure ground, a large, old-fashioned cottage, which has apparently been added to at different times by artistic hands that knew better than to destroy its original beauty. Protected by the great mountains from the wild, rough winds that blow up from St. George's Channel, the aspect of the cottage is such that even in mid-winter the whole is covered with roses and creepers which, clustering upwards, peep in at the bay-windows.

Nothing could be more disassociated with the scenes of death and battle than this quiet, peaceful spot; nevertheless, it bears the warlike name of Lordello, and was so called by the man who built it in memory of his brother, who fell in an engagement at the village of Lordello in Spain during the Peninsula war. But the place has been destined to have military surroundings, and is now the abode of Colonel Croker, lately retired from the service, and his talented wife, who is so well known to the world through her delightful novels of Indian life and experiences.

The tall, soldierly looking man who comes out into the hall has been a great traveller, and is a renowned *shikari*. The young girl yonder is their only child, and bears a striking resemblance to her father, with just a look of her mother, who is tall and very fair, with great Irish blue-grey eyes, in which a merry sparkle may be observed.

The interior of the cottage is all in keeping. The long, narrow hall, with two sitting-rooms on each side, is liberally decorated with tiger and leopard skins, Indian daggers, knives, horns and other trophies, whilst a magnificent stuffed tiger's head with gnashing teeth hangs over a door facing the entrance.

The pretty, bright drawing-room is daintily draped with silk embroideries from the East; the carpet was made at Agra; the piano has twice crossed the sea. Palms and ferns stand here and there among quaint Oriental carvings, brasses, and foreign ornaments of all sorts. On the walls hang several good water-colour sketches of places in India. Here a view of the blue hills of the Neilgherries, there scenes from the snow-covered Himalayan mountains.

Mrs. Croker's own little study has a French window opening onto the lawn, and has a warm, cheerful appearance with its bright-hued Indian carpet and easy-chairs, its great writing-table and bookcases. A good many novels can be detected behind its glass doors. "Hitherto," says Mrs. Croker, "I have had no means of knowing my fellow-workers except through their books. It is always a matter of regret to me that, living so much abroad, or in garrison towns at home, I have never had the opportunity of becoming personally acquainted with many of my own profession;

but in future I do hope to go occasionally to England and get into touch with those whose books I so much admire."

Mrs. Croker was born in Ireland, and comes of old Puritan families on both sides. Her father, the Rev. W. Sheppard, rector of Kilgefin, died in the prime of life when his only daughter was but seven years of age. He was a man of considerable intellectual attainments, a good writer and a brilliant conversationalist. The young girl was educated mostly in France, and being by nature a student, all her leisure hours were spent in reading. At school she distinguished herself by the fluency of her essays and the ease of her letter-writing, in which she depicted with equal reality the people whom she met and the places that she saw. History, geography, political and physical, poetry and languages, were her favourite studies, but arithmetic and algebra were alike repugnant. "Indeed, to be quite candid," says Mrs. Croker, laughing, "there used to be some sort of friendly exchange among the girls. Some, who were clever enough in other ways, would come to me in despair over a subject for a theme, such as 'Memory', 'Sympathy', and so on. I easily undertook their task and they in return too my algebra."

Accustomed from childhood to the saddle, her favourite recreation was riding; on her return from school she became a famous horsewoman and used to hunt with the Kildares. Shortly after she became engaged to Colonel Croker, of the Munster Fusiliers, then a lieutenant in the 21st Royal Scots Fusiliers, and when very young she married and immediately afterwards accompanied him to India.

Up to 1880 no idea of adopting literature as a profession had entered her head. She had never thought of writing a novel, still less of getting it published, but being naturally a close observer of places and of persons, she had accumulated a storehouse of information which was destined suddenly to be opened and drawn upon.

It happened that the "hot weather" of that year was abnormally hot; Secunderabad was more than usually scorched by the dry, arid winds of the Deccan. Ice was scarce, and even the incessant punkah day and night seemed to give no relief. The greater number of the residents had fled to the hills in search of cool breezes. Merely to amuse herself and to beguile the long weary days, she secretly drew out her pen. Then, as in a dream, everything passed swiftly before her: fleeting visions of places, people past and present, conversations, ideas, &c. The moment of inspiration had come and was seized; the hours now passed quickly enough; the intense heat—such as no one can imagine who has not passed a hot season in the plains—was forgotten, as day after day was spent in transmitting her thoughts to paper. But it was impossible wholly to conceal her occupation from the other ladies in the regiment, and after sundry veiled hints and delicate inquiries from her friends, Mrs. Croker, with many blushes, reluctantly revealed her secret and, after much persuasion, was prevailed upon to read aloud her MS.

"I called the book *Proper Pride*," says Mrs. Croker. "For many days we used to meet daily for these readings, but I never once thought of its finding its way into print. My friends kindly declared that it gave quite a new interest in their lives and unanimously pronounced that it ought to be published, but this was easier said than done. None of us had the slightest idea of how to set about getting a book printed. At last I sent it home to a publisher, and heard no more of it for a year; then, thinking that probably the parcel had been lost, I re-wrote the whole from memory."

Although this first effort had not as yet seen the light, the young author had become absorbed in the fascination of story-telling, and, nothing daunted, wrote her second work, *Pretty Miss Neville*, which again ran the gauntlet of her intimate friends, only in a series of private readings. In 1881 she and her husband went home regiment, and on their arrival the second MS. was sent to another firm of publishers. "I remember that it was Christmas Day," she reminisces—"I received an unwelcome Christmas-box in the shape of a most polite letter from the firm, and I can recall the very words in it: 'The story had no pretensions whatsoever to style or interest, and would not obtain even a passing notice from the public!' I was disheartened, but as my hopes had never been high, I was by no means a prey to despair. I supposed the verdict must be right, so I just put the whole MS. into a big grate where there was a fire smouldering and left the room. Luckily for me the fire was very low; my daughter, then a little girl, snatched it off and rescued it. She had heard the story read aloud and naturally thought a great deal of it. I then fell back on *Proper Pride*, which was not lost but only reposing with string uncut in the office where I had sent it, and it was eventually brought out. Needless to say, I was charmed to see myself in print, but I awaited with terror the reviews. I said to myself, that as long as a certain great weekly journal does not mention it at all I shall not so much mind, for I feared its ridicule."

But the author was needlessly alarmed. Her own modesty had led her to expect nothing more than an insignificant *début*, and she had scarcely even hoped that a mere amateur such as she considered herself would be noticed at all. She published anonymously, and no one was more surprised than she when the much-dreaded weekly devoted to the novel two columns of that meed of favourable criticism so dear to the heart of a writer. The principal daily paper too, and others, reviewed it equally pleasantly and nearly all the critics spoke of it as the work of a man. The book passed into three editions in six weeks. Like all Mrs. Croker's subsequent works, it has been translated into German, running previously through a German paper, and appeared simultaneously in Great Britain, in Australia, the United States and in Canada. It is now in its twelfth edition.

À propos of this book the author has a little anecdote to relate. So well had she concealed her identity that none of her friends in England had associated her with it. She was in the habit of hearing it frequently discussed at dinner parties and afternoon teas. One day she met an acquaintance at the Dover bookstall where they mutually subscribed. The lady, after mentioning the novel as being so popular and so widely read, remarked, "Someone actually told me that it was written by a Mrs. Croker in Dover, wife of an officer in the Royal Scots Fusiliers. Of course I laughed him to scorn. You are about the last person to write a book!" The author joined in the laugh. Presently the librarian came up and, bringing her own novel, whispered mysteriously, "I kept a copy aside for you as you are such a quick reader; there is a wonderful run on it. They say it is written by a lady in Dover." Mrs. Croker walked away with her book and made no remark.

Almost immediately after came the story that had been rescued from the flames, *Pretty Miss Neville*, which was even a greater success. It has lately been dramatised, and is shortly to be played in Vienna. This was followed at intervals of a year by *Someone Else*, *A Bird of Passage*, and *Diana Barrington*. These last two are the author's own favourites. Then came *Two Masters*, *Interference*, *A Family Likeness*, *"To Let"* (short stories), *A Third Person*, *The Poor Relation*, *Married Single*, and *The Real Lady Hilda*.

The delightful tales of India are studies from life. The descriptions of scenery so graphically and artistically given are all true backgrounds to the stories. The natives are all real persons and described as the author saw them. She has indeed had peculiar opportunities for becoming so intimately acquainted with India. Owing to exceptional circumstances, she had been enabled to travel over the greater part of the country. Exclusive of trips home, Mrs. Croker has spent about fourteen years in the East, and has seen nearly the whole of the Madras Presidency, Burmah, the Andamans, the Deccan, and the Neilgherries,

This long residence was not, however, altogether of their own choice. Colonel Croker had done one tour of India and then spent a few years at home when he was placed on half-pay, owing to one of the many Royal Warrants. He was subsequently brought into another regiment and despatched on a second tour to the East, when they visited most of the Central and North-West Provinces.

Of the Neilgherries the author speaks with much enthusiasm. She "has an admiration almost amounting to a passion for these Blue Hills", and declares them to be in all respects the most delightful and salubrious of ranges". As she journeyed up, "the close, tropical vegetation was left behind, the trees assumed a more European aspect, the air lost its steamy feel and became every instant more rarefied and pure. The path appeared to wind in and out through mountain-sides clothed with trees and foliage of every description. A foaming river was tearing headlong down a wide, rocky channel and taking frantic leaps over all impediments. Wild roses and wild geraniums abounded on all sides; enormous benches of heliotrope were growing between the stones; lovely flowering creepers connected the trees. Before the windows of the hotel there was a hedge of heliotrope cut like box at me, so high and so dense that you could ride on one side of it and someone else on the other without either being aware of mutual proximity. It was one mass of flowers, and smelt like ten thousand cherry-pies, and was one of the sights of the Neilgherries; but for actual grandeur and magnificence of scenery even these hills cannot be compared to the Himalayas."

Loving the beauties of Nature before all things, and having enjoyed the advantages of living amidst some of the finest scenery in the world, Mrs. Croker is peculiarly happy in her brilliant and vivid word-painting of the places she depicts. The reader can see with his own eyes the views that she describes. He feels himself to be one of those present whether in the home-life of a bungalow in the plains, or in the gay society of a fashionable hill-station in these most attractive and interesting pictures of life in India. He makes one of the group of passengers on board the P. and O. steamer, one of the party at the exciting tiger-hunts and pig-sticking adventures. The reason is not far to seek. There is an atmosphere of reality about her books. The very animals of which she writes seem to have an individuality of their own. The brightness and crispness of the dialogue cause each character to stand out and contribute its share to the development of the story.

She is equally at home in the description of fox-hunting in Ireland as in her race meeting and sporting scenes in India, and a reader would imagine that she must have been present at many a tiger-hunt, but this is not the case. Colonel Croker was, however, a keen sportsman and his experiences came in quite fresh to her; but this would not be enough without special faculty of observation and the gift of forcibly expressing so much in so few words that constitute the charm of Mrs. Croker's writing. The stories are told simply and with much vivacity. The most telling situations are concisely narrated and the interest is never allowed to flag. Certainly, she was never present on a field of battle, yet her stirring account of the Afghanistan expedition, and the camp-life of the troops in South Africa, are related with so much spirit and veracity that those who, in the flesh, took part in both can vouch for their fidelity.

"There were a few things that were only too real to me," says Mrs. Croker. "I have twice been in the camp when a tiger has been in the neighbourhood, and seen the mark of his pugs, after he had carried off a pet dog. Once a panther took a dear little dog out of the verandah of our bungalow, and I have often, to my sorrow, been up and down the six hundred steps described in *Diana Barrington*, when we were at Ram Tek dâk Bungalow. It was the only means of getting down to the water. Ram Tek is a wonderful place, quite off the beaten track and but little known."

Mrs. Croker has a volume of native stories and a new Indian novel in hand, which has, indeed, been on the stocks for two years. All are sketched out in the rough from copious notes taken on the spot. She never writes in haste, and finds it so hard to please herself that often one chapter is re-written ten times before it is allowed to pass. Her working hours are generally in the early morning, for she preserves the habit acquired in India of being up betimes. When deeply engrossed in a story and in writing mood, she is often known to work for ten or twelve hours for many consecutive days, until the people who are worrying her brain are drawn in black and white; but then someone in authority is apt to intervene, and his slightest wish is her law. She loves writing for its own sake, even if it were never to produce a penny. Luckily, however, it brings in a good many pennies; but she maintains that the greatest pleasure she derives from it consists in the receipt of many letters from strangers and invalids, often at the other end of the world, saying that her books have wiled away many a long and weary hour of sickness, or have produced much temporary distraction and comfort when in anxiety or in sorrow.

With all her experiences of sport at home and abroad, Mrs. Croker is essentially gentle and feminine in her tastes and habits. She is bright and frank in manner, with a pretty wit, for which her Irish blood is partly responsible. She has plenty of practical good sense, and a happy, sunny nature which looks on things from the brightest point of view. Her concluding words are thoroughly characteristic. "The press," she observes, with much feeling, "on which I do not know a soul, has always treated me most generously, and much of my encouragement has come from my unknown critics, to whom I am truly grateful."

Hindi and Urdu Glossary

Anna—Unit of currency

Baboo—A respectful term accorded a Hindu gentleman or official

Bandy—A carriage usually drawn by a bullock

Bhootia Bungalow—A haunted bungalow

Burra sahib—Chief companion

Charpoy—Native bed

Chowkidar (or *Chokedar*)—Watchman

Chotah hazra—Meal served at dawn

Chuprassie—Wearer of an official badge, especially an attendant occupying an important position in the households of Indian landowners

Coolie—An unskilled labourer

Dacoit—Armed bandit

Dâk—A system of mail delivery of passenger transport by relays or bearers of horses stations at intervals along a route

Dâk Bungalow—A house where travellers on a dâk route could be accommodated

Dhobie—A caste with traditional occupation as a clothes washer

Dirzee—A tailor

Dothi—A long loincloth typically worn by men

Ekka—Small one-horsed vehicle

Gharry—Horse-drawn vehicle available for hire

Ghaut (or *Ghat*)—Mountain pass; or valley in a mountain range

Jampanies—Rickshaw bearers

Jawarri (or *Jawari*, *Jowari*)—Millet, extensively culti-
vated in India

Jheel—A pond or wetland area

Khana—Food; a meal

Khansamah—House-steward; a native male servant,
usually the head of the kitchen

Khitmatgar—Native male servant, usually the caretaker

Khud—Deep ravine or chasm; a precipitous cleft or
descent on a hillside

Khuskhus—Aromatic perennial Indian grass, whose roots
are woven into mats, fans, and baskets

Khuskhus tatties—Cooling method that employs mats
made of khuskhus grass

Koss—Unit of measurement; roughly three kilometres
or two miles

Kutcha—Makeshift, ramshackle; antonym of pucka

Mallee (or *Mali*)—Native gardener

Mem-sahib—A European woman of high social standing,
particularly a British official's wife

Nabob—Term for native Europeans who make their
fortunes abroad, typically in India

Nautch—A popular dance performed by young women

Phoolkari (or *Phulkari*)—Flower embroidery; a cloth or
shawl so embroidered

Pucka—Solid, built with permanence; antonym of kutcha.

Punkah—Hand-operated ceiling fan

Ryot—A peasant cultivator

Serai—Inn

Shikari—Big game hunter or professional guide

Soucar—Hindu banker or moneylender

Ticca Gharry—Hired carriage

Tiffin—Snack or a light meal

Tonga—Light two-wheeled vehicle

Topee—Pith helmet

Acknowledgements

This volume was originally published by Sarob Press as the third instalment in their "Mistresses of the Macabre" series, edited by Richard Dalby.

I am thankful to those who assisted with this previous edition: Michael Flowers, Michael Gill, Crispin Jackson, Sara Morgan, Ben Whitaker, and Paul Lowe. I am particularly indebted to Robert Morgan; and, of course, to the friendship and undying scholarship of the late Richard Dalby.

I would also like to extend my gratitude, for this new edition, to the Estate of Richard Dalby: Jean and Joe Conway, and Mark Conway; to Alan Corbett for his excellent cover art, and to the Swan River team: Meggan Kehrli, Ken Mackenzie, and Jim Rockhill. Finally, I would like to thank Alison Lyons of Dublin UNESCO City of Literature and Dublin City Libraries for their continued support.

"Number Ninety" and Other Ghost Stories
was originally published by
Sarob Press, Mountain Ash, Wales (2000).

❀

"Number Ninety" was first published in *Chapman's Magazine of Fiction*, Christmas 1895; a slightly revised version, retitled "An Unexpected Invitation", appeared in *A State Secret* (Methuen, 1901).

"To Let" was first published in *London Society*, Christmas Number 1890; it was collected in *"To Let"* (London: Chatto & Windus, 1893).

"The Dâk Bungalow at Dakor" was first published in *London Society* in 1882; it was collected in *"To Let"* (London: Chatto & Windus, 1893).

"The Former Passengers", "If You See Her Face", and "The Khitmagar" appeared in *"To Let"* (London: Chatto & Windus, 1893).

"Her Last Wishes" and "The First Comer" appeared in *In the Kingdom of Kerry and Other Stories* (London: Chatto & Windus, 1896).

"Trooper Thompson's Information" and "Mrs. Ponsonby's Dream" appeared in *Jason and Other Stories* (London: Chatto & Windus, 1899).

"Who Knew the Truth?", "La Carcassone", and "The Door Ajar" appeared in *The Old Cantonment with Other Stories of India and Elsewhere* (London: Methuen, 1905).

"The Red Bungalow" and "The North Verandah" appeared in *Odds and Ends* (London: Hutchinson, 1919).

"Mrs. Croker" appeared in *Pen, Pencil, Baton and Mask: Biographical Sketches* (London: Spottiswoode, 1896).

About the Author

B. M. Croker was born in Co. Roscommon in 1849. She married John Stokes Croker, an officer in the Royal Scots Fusiliers, in 1870, and accompanied him to India, there commencing a long literary career. Authoring some fifty-two books, including *Pretty Miss Neville* (1883), *Infatuation* (1899), and *The Pagoda Tree* (1919), her novel *The Road to Mandalay* was filmed in 1926. Mrs. Croker died at a nursing home in London, after a short and sudden illness, on 20 October 1920.

About the Editor

Richard Dalby (1949-2017), born in London, was a widely-respected editor, anthologist, and scholar of supernatural fiction. He has edited collections by E. F. Benson, Bram Stoker, and Rosa Mulholland; and his numerous anthologies include *Dracula's Brood*, *Victorian Ghost Stories by Eminent Women Writers*, and *Victorian and Edwardian Ghost Stories*.

BENDING TO EARTH
Strange Stories by Irish Women

edited by Maria Giakaniki
and Brian J. Showers

Irish women have long produced literature of the gothic, uncanny, and supernatural. *Bending to Earth* draws together twelve such tales. While none of the authors herein were considered primarily writers of fantastical fiction during their lifetimes, they each wandered at some point in their careers into more speculative realms—some only briefly, others for lengthier stays.

Names such as Charlotte Riddell and Rosa Mulholland will already be familiar to aficionados of the eerie, while Katharine Tynan and Clotilde Graves are sure to gain new admirers. From a ghost story in the Swiss Alps to a premonition of death in the West of Ireland to strange rites in a South Pacific jungle, *Bending to Earth* showcases a diverse range of imaginative writing which spans the better part of a century.

"Bending to Earth *is full of tales of women walled-up in rooms, of vengeful or unforgetting dead wives, of mistreated lovers, of cruel and murderous husbands.*"

– Darryl Jones, *Irish Times*

"*A surprising, extraordinary anthology featuring twelve uncanny and supernatural stories from the nineteenth century . . . highly recommended, extremely enjoyable.*"

– *British Fantasy Society*

NOT TO BE TAKEN
AT BED-TIME
and Other Strange Stories

Rosa Mulholland

In the late-nineteenth century Rosa Mulholland (1841-1921) achieved great popularity and acclaim for her many novels, written for both an adult audience and younger readers. Several of these novels chronicled the lives of the poor, often incorporating rural Irish settings and folklore. Earlier in her career, Mulholland became one of the select band of authors employed by Charles Dickens to write stories for his popular magazine *All the Year Round*, together with Wilkie Collins, Elizabeth Gaskell, Joseph Sheridan Le Fanu, and Amelia B. Edwards.

Mulholland's best supernatural and weird short stories have been gathered together in the present collection, edited and introduced by Richard Dalby, to celebrate this gifted late Victorian "Mistress of the Macabre".

"It's a mark of a good writer that they can be immersed in the literary culture of their time and yet manage to transcend it, and Mulholland does that with the tales collected here."

– David Longhorn, *Supernatural Tales*

THE DEATH SPANCEL
and Others

Katharine Tynan

Katharine Tynan is not a name immediately associated with the supernatural. However, like many other writers of the early twentieth century, she made numerous forays into literature of the ghostly and macabre, and throughout her career produced verse and prose that conveys a remarkable variety of eerie themes, moods, and narrative forms. From her early, elegiac stories, inspired by legends from the West of Ireland, to pulpier efforts featuring grave-robbers and ravenous rats, Tynan displays an eye for weird detail, compelling atmosphere, and a talent for rendering a broad palette of uncanny effects. *The Death Spancel and Others* is the first collection to showcase Tynan's tales of supernatural events, prophecies, curses, apparitions, and a pervasive sense of the ghastly.

"Of remarkably high literary quality . . . a great collection recommended to any good fiction lover."

– Mario Guslandi

"Tynan's fiction is of a high standard, crafted in relatively simple yet still lyrical prose . . . a very assured craftswoman of the supernatural tale."

– Supernatural Tales

"Lovers of late Victorian and Edwardian ghost fiction will assuredly adore the restrained literary quality . . ."

– The Pan Review

CPSIA information can be obtained
at www.ICGtesting.com
Printed in the USA
BVHW072047240921
617497BV00003B/147